STALKED ... BY A SPIRIT!

Slocum led his horse into the saloon and began unpacking his saddlebags when a bolt of lightning split the sky.

Slocum blinked, thinking he saw a tall, bedslat-thin man with arms crossed over his chest standing on the far side of the street, watching him intently.

When a second lightning bolt lit up Buzzard Flats, the man had vanished.

Shaking it off, he spread his bedroll and lay down. He had just drifted off to sleep when he heard the planking near the door creak once . . .

This book also contains a special preview of
Texas Horsetrading Co.,
the exciting new Western novel by
Gene Shelton.

DON'T MISS THESE
ALL-ACTION WESTERN SERIES
FROM THE BERKLEY PUBLISHING GROUP

***THE GUNSMITH** by J. R. Roberts*
Clint Adams was a legend among lawmen, outlaws, and ladies. They called him . . . the Gunsmith.

***LONGARM** by Tabor Evans*
The popular long-running series about U.S. Deputy Marshal Long—his life, his loves, his fight for justice.

***LONE STAR** by Wesley Ellis*
The blazing adventures of Jessica Starbuck and the martial arts master, Ki. Over eight million copies in print.

***SLOCUM** by Jake Logan*
Today's longest-running action Western. John Slocum rides a deadly trail of hot blood and cold steel.

GHOST TOWN

BERKLEY BOOKS, NEW YORK

If you purchased this book without a cover, you should be aware that this book is stolen property. It was reported as "unsold and destroyed" to the publisher, and neither the author nor the publisher has received any payment for this "stripped book."

GHOST TOWN

A Berkley Book / published by arrangement with
the author

PRINTING HISTORY
Berkley edition / March 1994

All rights reserved.
Copyright © 1994 by The Berkley Publishing Group.
Texas Horsetrading Co. by Gene Shelton copyright © 1994 by
Charter Communications, Inc.
This book may not be reproduced in whole
or in part, by mimeograph or any other means,
without permission. For information address:
The Berkley Publishing Group,
200 Madison Avenue,
New York, New York 10016.

ISBN: 0-425-14128-4

BERKLEY®
Berkley Books are published by The Berkley Publishing Group,
200 Madison Avenue,
New York, New York 10016.
BERKLEY and the "B" design are trademarks
belonging to Berkley Publishing Corporation.

PRINTED IN THE UNITED STATES OF AMERICA

10 9 8 7 6 5 4 3 2 1

GHOST TOWN

1

The Wyoming rain refused to let up. Slocum pulled his battered wide-brimmed Stetson down further on his forehead to protect his eyes, but this didn't let him see any better. The wind whipping up the lush, green V-shaped valley splashed the rain into his face, no matter how he turned or twisted. Bending lower over his Appaloosa's neck didn't help, either. He was wet, tired, and about ready to go to ground and let the squall blow itself out. Weather in late spring was always unpredictable, especially west of Bent's Fort and heading into the high mountains west of South Pass.

Before Slocum could rein back and seek out shelter, his horse stumbled on slippery ground. He shifted in his saddle to keep the Appaloosa on all four feet, but this didn't work. His horse's back legs folded up under its belly as the entire side of the trail gave way.

"Yeow!" Slocum cried as he fought to stay on his horse, falling more than riding down the hillside. A mud slide like this was treacherous because he had no idea how far he was going to slide. As he had meandered around scouting a trail for the wagon train five miles behind him, he had passed more than one, hundred-foot drop. If the infernal rain hadn't blinded

2   JAKE LOGAN

him so, he would know if he was headed over one now.

A limb suddenly came out of the driving rain and smashed into his face, knocking him to one side. Slocum's strong legs kept him in the saddle, but he threw the Appaloosa off balance and the horse fell to its left, pinning Slocum's leg under its weight.

Slocum grunted in pain and then the horse vanished from sight, sliding faster downhill as it struggled. He heard the shrill neighing as the frightened Appaloosa disappeared into the storm. Slocum fought to get to his feet but his bruised leg, the torrents of mud rushing around him on its way downhill, and the heavy rain robbed him of balance. He somersaulted twice in the thick mud and then began sliding on his belly, headfirst down the slope.

Slocum threw his arms up over the top of his head to keep from bashing his brains out on a rock or another tree. He stayed in this position long seconds after he came to a stop, more dazed than hurt from his long fall. Wiping mud from his face, he slipped around until he got to his feet. The rain had let up a little, giving him a few yards visibility. He saw the black-and-white spotted blanket on his Appaloosa's rump and whistled loudly.

The frightened horse turned in the direction of its master, eyes wide with fear. Slocum whistled again, and the horse settled down a mite. Slogging through the ankle-deep mud, Slocum reached the horse's side and began soothing it, talking in a low voice as he checked all four legs for any damage. The horse had survived the fall better than its rider.

"Come on, old fella," Slocum said softly, tugging on the reins to get the horse moving toward a small grove of trees. The lodgepole pines might not provide much shelter, but it was better than standing in the middle of the downpour.

"We can ride out the storm," Slocum said, wiping mud off the still-spooked animal. "It's not coming down anywhere near as hard now. Calm down and we'll look for some food." Slocum led the Appaloosa to a thick tuft of grass and let the horse graze. Then he tended to himself, wiping off a thick layer of mud and finally sitting with his back to a tree, blocking out most of the rain. He pulled off his left boot and rolled up the canvas pants leg to examine his bruises. Bright green and purple spots showed where he had been caught and dragged under the Appaloosa, but gentle probing showed Slocum he hadn't broken any bones. He rubbed the flesh and flinched, but he knew he was still in one piece, even if he wasn't entirely fit as a fiddle.

Slocum closed his eyes a moment and rested, wondering how the blazes he had gotten himself into this job. The answer kept coming back to haunt him. He had agreed to scout for the wagon train because the wagon master was an old friend. Benjamin Carter had pulled Slocum's fat out of the fire a couple years back, and Slocum owed him.

But how much? How long did he have to endure the spring storms, the treacherous mountain passes, and the ungrateful people making up Carter's train? More than once he had been ordered about like a servant to the high falutin'. That had rankled more than anything else. He owed Carter and was more than willing to repay a debt, but Slocum considered himself the equal of any man in the wagon train, no matter what they'd paid for their wagons, teams, or possessions.

Slocum snorted. He was more than the equal to most of them. He was—or had been—a fair farmer when he and his family had lived back in Calhoun, Georgia. Only the war had changed his intentions of settling down and farming Slocum's Stand. The land had been in the family since the original grant from George I, and only a carpetbagger judge had changed that.

Slocum's right hand tensed slightly, as if circling the butt of his ebony-handled Colt Navy slung at his left hip in a worn cross-draw holster. He had ridden with Quantrill's Raiders in Kansas and hadn't gotten along too good with the guerrillas in the vicious band after the Lawrence, Kansas, massacre. Bill Anderson had taken special glee in gut-shooting Slocum for protesting the murder of women and children. By the time Slocum had recuperated, the war was over and he had made his way home to find the judge hankering after the entire valley where the Slocum family's five hundred acres spread all green and peaceful.

No taxes had been paid, the judge said, and he had a hired gun to back up his claim. Slocum had ridden away from the buildings he had deliberately set afire—and the two fresh graves up near where the spring house had been. That judge-killing charge had dogged his steps through the West ever since.

"Almost better being hanged than putting up with those sodbusters," Slocum grumbled. He peered out from under the brim of his hat and saw the storm breaking up. Lightning still cracked and rumbled over the distant mountains, but the clouds opened up enough to show patches of bright blue Wyoming sky.

Slocum heaved to his feet and went to his Appaloosa. His leg still throbbed from the fall he had taken, but he didn't think it would give him much trouble after the weather dried up a mite. Climbing stiffly into the saddle, Slocum set about doing his scout down along the canyon floor. Within two miles, valley walls pinched down hard into a rocky ravine that would give Carter a devil of a time getting his wagon train through. In spite of the rain showers, the river in the center of the boulder-strewn area wasn't too swollen at the moment, but Slocum saw from the water marks on the sheer walls how dangerous the passage might be. After an hour's hunting, Slocum decided there wasn't any better way up the valley.

It took the better part of the day for him to finish his scouting and then backtrack to find the wagon train. He heaved a sigh when he saw the ragged line of canvas-topped wagons making their way alongside the run-off swollen stream.

They had forded the Snake River and had been crossing and recrossing every tributary feeding that mighty flow for two days. It was nothing short of a miracle that none of the wagons had been lost to the swift waters.

Slocum acknowledged Carter's wave and rode to the front of the train where the wagon master rode on his swaybacked sorrel. How the poor animal managed to keep stumbling along was a mystery Slocum didn't want to poke into. In a way, the horse was like its rider. Benjamin Carter might not move or talk fast, but he never stopped. Like a slow drip, he kept going until he got to where he was going.

"John, we got problems," Carter said without so much as a howdy-do.

"The way ahead's clear for another day, maybe two," Slocum said. "I didn't see any place you couldn't ford."

"What's ahead isn't as troublesome as what's behind," Carter said. The wagon master whipped off his battered black bowler and wiped his forehead on his sleeve. He slumped in the saddle and looked a dozen years older than he had before Slocum had left the wagon train. Thick lines were plowed across Carter's forehead, and he had a curious pallor that, in another man, might mean long months spent out of the sun. Slocum knew better. Carter was always tending his flock of sodbusters like a sheep dog tending his flock.

"You look like hell," Slocum said. "What happened? We're not being chased down by Cheyenne, are we? I thought I saw some sign a day or two back, but I thought it was a hunting party and they were heading north, not west."

"No Injuns," Carter said. "I wish it was as simple as that." He wiped his face again, the sweat popping up as soon as he finished the motion. "Yes, sir, Indians would be a sight better. It's that damnfool Immanuel Stoner."

Slocum knew the man and had crossed him more than once. The only reason Slocum bothered riding anywhere near the Stoner party was their daughter Sarah. Slocum might have set eyes on a prettier filly in his day, but he wasn't sure exactly when or where.

Her old man was a different matter. Immanuel Stoner was bullheaded and couldn't be told anything. Stoner might have been a fair farmer—and from the look of his expensive wagons and yokes of oxen, he had been very successful back in Missouri—but he didn't know squat about travelling across country. Slocum didn't care much for Stoner's son, David, either. The boy had developed a mean streak somewhere along the way. And the way Mrs. Stoner stared at him, never saying a word, but always watching with her pale gray eyes like Slocum had seen once in a cadaver, made him feel as if he'd just stomped barefooted on a fresh egg.

"What's he up to now?" asked Slocum. He stood in the stirrups and let his green eyes count back along the line of wagons. Stoner insisted on being at the end of the wagon train, for whatever reason. But when Slocum came up two wagons shy, he settled back down in the saddle. He feared what Carter was going to say.

"We was fordin' the stream back about three hours ago," Carter said. "I wasn't payin' much attention since ole Mrs. Wallens was having trouble with her rig. Two of the other fellas helped her along, and I thought we was all across."

"But not the Stoner party," Slocum finished. Carter shook his head sadly, giving Slocum all the answer he needed. "Where do you reckon they got off to?"

"There was a branching canyon. Stoner might have taken off down it, thinkin' it was a short cut. He was giving me all kinds of grief 'bout the number of times we was havin' to ford the river. I tried to tell him why we done it like we did. I did!"

"How that man's ever going to reach Oregon is beyond me," Slocum said. He had let Carter spin the tale in his own roundabout, slow as molasses way, but he knew time worked against them. The only chance the Stoners had of staying alive for long was to get back in line with the other wagons. The Cheyenne party Slocum had seen days before might come back or a war party might come boiling out of the south. Ever since Custer had massacred Black Kettle at Washita Creek, the Cheyenne had been raising all kinds of mayhem.

Not that Slocum blamed them much. Black Kettle had tried to keep the peace, but Custer was out to make a reputation. Slocum had heard the "boy general" had a real hankering for a Congressional Medal like the pair his brother, Tom, had won during the war at Namozine Church, Virginia, and later at Sayler's Creek. Since his court martial, there wasn't a hound's chance in hell of that, but Custer wasn't one to give up easily.

"You want me to go fetch them?" Slocum was already settling in the saddle for the ride. He wanted to rest his Appaloosa but knew that wasn't likely to happen for quite a spell. If Carter had lost the Stoner party three hours back, that meant at least an hour's ride. Slocum didn't know how hard it would be to track the wagons once he found where the sodbusters had split off from the main party, but he wasn't anticipating much trouble. The huge Conestogas left deep ruts that a blind man could find with one hand tied behind his back.

"I'll get the wagon train along as far as I can before sundown, but we won't go off without word of what happened to 'em," Carter promised.

"Keep an eye on the sky," cautioned Slocum. "There's more rain up there." He jerked his thumb in the direction of new clouds of leaden gray boiling over the mountains. It didn't look as if the wagons had been through much of a shower, but the stream was boiling and swollen from the earlier storm.

"You know me, John. I worry about every little damned thing." Carter smiled weakly and motioned Slocum on his way. Carter settled his derby back square on his head and rode off, grumbling to himself. Slocum waved to a few of the people in the train as he rode past, but most of them only glared at him, as if every hardship they endured was his personal problem. By the time the end of the wagon train was behind him, Slocum was considering how Carter would feel if he just kept on riding.

But Slocum wouldn't do that. Benjamin Carter was a friend, and Slocum's sense of honor prevented him from abandoning him like that. When they got to trail's end, though, was another matter. Slocum intended to turn north and head up into Washington and maybe find a companion horse to his Appaloosa. A pair might give him breeding stock. A dozen would do even better. Raising a herd of the sturdy, dependable horses and selling them would go a long ways toward putting real money in Slocum's pocket, money that Carter could never pay for scouting.

8   JAKE LOGAN

Slocum rode along, drifting, not paying much attention to the countryside. After he almost passed the wagon train's last ford, he snapped out of his reverie. The gentle, even motion of the horse had lulled him into a trance. He dismounted and studied the torn-up ground where the wagons had come across, wondering why Carter had picked this spot to ford. He had told the wagon master to cross a half mile farther down.

Shaking his head, Slocum stood and looked across the broad stream—river. He couldn't call this a stream when it was this wide and fast-running. Slocum started to mount when he heard a crack of thunder. He took a good look to the sky for the first time since coming back to find the Stoners and saw the heavy storm clouds and didn't like what he saw.

Slocum wished he had given Carter a better idea what lay ahead of the wagon train. Instead, the Stoners' plight had occupied his mind, as it had Carter's. The valley narrowed only a mile or two from where Slocum had left the wagons. Given the time it had taken to ride back, Carter must have reached that rocky neck by now. Any rain higher up in the valley would wash through the narrows in a flood that would sweep even the heaviest wagon away.

Slocum looked across the tributary and then back up the valley toward the formidable rain clouds. He could cross and chase after the Stoners or he could return and warn Carter what he was getting into. Slocum cursed himself for a fool because he hadn't done that when he'd had the chance.

Mounted, he glanced across the river, then turned and retraced his path in the direction of the wagon train. He had to warn Carter of the danger. Immanuel Stoner and his family could fend for themselves, just a while longer. If they were on the other side of the river and heading up a canyon without a stream pouring down its middle, they wouldn't be in anywhere near the trouble the wagon train might find.

Slocum pushed the Appaloosa to its limit returning. And his worst fears were realized when he saw that Carter had inexplicably called the wagon train to a halt in the very draw that would turn into a deathtrap if the water rose much more.

He galloped up, shouting for the wagon master. From near the front of the train he saw the man's rounded black bowler bobbing about.

"Carter, you can't stop here. This whole flat's going to be underwater if that storm gets any worse." Slocum pointed to the northwest. "You have to get another mile before the valley widens again."

"Can't help it, John," answered Carter, wiping his face with a greasy rag that left streaks on his face. Carter tucked the rag back into a pocket and pointed. An axle had broken on the leading wagon and held up the others.

"Get the rest of the train moving," Slocum ordered. "I'll see what I can do here. I have a bad feeling about this storm."

"Don't go gettin' a case of nerves on me, John. I need you steady and true," Carter said. The man blinked when a clap of thunder rolled along the valley and through the rocky narrows. He looked up at either side and saw the tall cliffs. If possible, he turned even whiter as he realized the position he had put the wagon train in.

"Go on now," Slocum said. "I'll do what I can." He jumped to the ground and wiggled under the wagon. Two men in the wagon held a long pole, levering the back up. Their women stood nearby, anxiously chattering among themselves.

Slocum saw that the axle was broken beyond repair. The wheels needed to be yanked off and a new axle turned. Slipping from under the wagon he motioned for the men to relax. They lowered the wagon, which sagged precariously to one side.

"How long'll it take to fix?" asked the oldest of the men, hardly twenty years old if he was a day. He looked uneasily as the other wagons rattled past.

Slocum wasn't paying as much attention to the wagon train as he was to the building storm. Thunder blasted down the ravine in noisy cannonade. And where there was that kind of noise, there had to be a whale-load of rain being dumped from the sky.

"You folks know anyone else in the train willing to give you a hand?" Slocum pulled back the canvas flap and saw the heavy cargo inside. The other wagons were as fully loaded and had scant room for this much furniture and farming equipment.

"Might be one or two," the man allowed, scratching his head. "Nobody's got a spare axle that I know of."

"I was thinking more of taking what you can salvage from here. Your clothes and personal items," Slocum said.

"What are you saying, Mr. Slocum?" demanded the man's wife, a thin, plain girl of hardly seventeen. "You can't mean for us to abandon our wagon and belongings!"

Slocum cocked his head to one side and heard something more than the crash of thunder. He couldn't be sure with the wagon train passing by, but he thought the ground shook—just like it might if a wall of water was rushing down the valley.

"I don't rightly know, but you might not have much time, Miz Dunleavy. Get what you can carry and hop onto another wagon. If there's no flood, we can come back and repair the wagon."

"But—" She turned to her young husband to protest.

Slocum spun and shouted to the wagon master, "Roll 'em hard and fast, Carter! That's a flash flood coming down the valley!"

The water was rising fast in the river and would sweep away the whole train in another few minutes unless they reached the safety that lay past the rocky constriction in the valley walls.

2

"My kitchen utensils!" the young wife cried, starting for her broken down wagon. Slocum never hesitated. He took two quick steps, got his arm around the woman's thin waist and swung her about. Mrs. Dunleavy fought, but Slocum ignored the bony fists pounding on his shoulder and arm as he threw her belly down over his saddle.

"Get onto the other wagons and whip the teams!" Slocum saw that the woman's husband was slow to react, not understanding what was happening. The three men with him were similarly confused and didn't see the danger. Slocum put his heels into the Appaloosa's flanks and got the horse trotting off briskly. The young man yelled a protest, then came running after Slocum and his wife, laying over the saddle pommel and kicking fiercely.

"Keep those wagons moving," Slocum repeated, drawing his six-shooter. He started firing to get the teams spooked enough to pull their heavy loads. Because of the high cliffs on either side of the river, it wouldn't do to abandon the wagons and teams and strike out on foot. The wagon train's only hope lay in getting out of the rocky ravine before the water rose too much.

"Stop, come back, you can't do this!" The man pounding hard after him almost caught up. Slocum urged the horse to more speed and left the man behind.

Slocum fired again when he saw the water beginning to overflow the rocky banks and rise quickly. The heavy rains higher on the mountain slopes had finally come flooding down, heightened by even more water from the heavy showers kicking up again. His Colt Navy came up empty and he thrust the six-gun back into his holster, fighting to keep the woman from sliding off the horse and hurting herself.

"Calm down, will you!" he said irritably. Slocum worried that the last of the wagons might not clear the rocky, narrow ravine before the real rush of the flash flood came tearing down on them. The woman refused to lie still, so he heaved and dumped her to the ground.

"Your husband'll be along in a few minutes," he told her, accepting her angry glare as payment for saving her life. "You get on up to high ground the best you can."

"Our wagon's back there. Everything we own is in that wagon!"

"You've still got your life. Be content with that." Slocum wheeled about and went to urge the oxen on the last wagon to greater speed. He thanked his lucky stars that no one used burros or mules. Those cantankerous animals might decide simply to stop and doom their drivers. Oxen could be coaxed into motion, given liberal use of a whip.

The rush of water almost deafened him as he leaned over and used his spurs on an ox's hindquarter. The bull let out a snort and pulled all the harder to come after Slocum. This pulled the wagon far enough from the rising river to save both wagon and family cowering inside.

"You folks all right?" Slocum called. The man in the driver's box nodded, his mouth working like a fish out of water. Slocum trotted back until he got a good look into the rocky draw, now filled from side to side. Anyone caught in that frantic rush of water from the high mountains would have been drowned for sure. He let his Appaloosa back away, then struggled up a shale slope to join Benjamin Carter.

The wagon master had his hands full with Mrs. Dunleavy and her husband, already complaining about Slocum.

"He made us leave our wagon!" the young man protested. "We're flat busted now. We lost everything back there because he wouldn't help us!"

"Seems that Mr. Slocum saved your lives," Carter said in his slow drawl. "Ain't no kerosene lamp or fancy-ass carved table what's worth the life of a fine woman like Mrs. Dunleavy, now is there, sir?" Carter cocked his head to one side and studied the indignant man.

Slocum saw that the other three with the Dunleavy party were straggling up the slope, looking like drowned rats. They had escaped, but barely. Slocum urged the Appaloosa around behind Carter and saw that the survivors on the wagon train had pulled into a meadow and were already busy repairing the damage done by the dash through the narrow canyon.

"He made us lose everything," Dunleavy insisted. "He owes us. We could'a fixed that there axle. We could'a saved our gear. We even lost our team!"

The other three joined the chorus demanding that Slocum put things right. Carter heaved a sigh and turned to Slocum, motioning him to one side.

"John, you done good, but you can see how it is with these folks."

"I'll go find the Stoner party and get them back into the fold," Slocum said, knowing Carter was right. His services were better employed at a distance to let the Dunleavys cool off a mite. "It's going to be a spell before that water recedes enough to let me get through the canyon, though. The Stoners might end up a couple days behind the rest of the train."

"Cain't be helped," Carter said. Louder, he said, "You get on out of here, Mr. Slocum. You got work to do back there." With this public dismissal, Carter turned back to the Dunleavys and spent a few more minutes soothing their ruffled feathers.

Slocum didn't wait around to hear the outcome. He wouldn't have Carter's job as wagon master for all the gold in California. Slocum preferred dealing with cantankerous horses, not people.

If he hadn't been riding out, he was as likely to have punched Dunleavy as listened to his complaints. The young fool and his scrawny bride couldn't see that he had saved their lives, and the lives of the three men with them.

Fuming as he rode, Slocum found a spot a mile away from the wagon train. He knew Carter might decide to camp there for a day or so to be sure that the treacherous river wasn't going to flood again and take out more of his paying customers. But that didn't lessen the feeling Slocum had that finding Immanuel Stoner and his family had to be done fast. Stoner could travel quite a ways and there was no telling the kind of devilment he could get into.

Slocum stretched out under a tree, waiting for the river to recede. As he half-dozed, he thought about Sarah Stoner. She seemed to favor him, in spite of her father's disapproval. But then Slocum wasn't sure Immanuel Stoner would approve of any suitor. He had the look of a man born contrary and downright mean.

Slocum came awake with a start just a bit after sundown. The cold wind whipping down the valley alerted him that the weather was shifting again, but a quick look at the river showed how the flood waters had abated enough for him to make his way along the rocky edge and return for the Stoners.

Heaving himself to his feet, Slocum found his patient Appaloosa and mounted. He rode slowly along the river's edge, then made better time when he got to the far eastern end of the rocky draw. Before midnight he had returned to the spot where Carter had brought his wagon train across the rapidly flowing river—and where the Stoner party had refused to ford.

"Here we go," Slocum said, urging his horse into the river. The storms hadn't dumped any more water into the river, and he forded with little effort. Even a fully-laden wagon with a team of oxen pulling could have made it across. There was no reason for Stoner to have refused to follow the others.

He dismounted on the far side and dried the horse the best he could. The cold wind would chill the Appaloosa, and Slocum guessed he had a ways to travel before resting. Walking slowly, he backtracked on the wagon train for more than an hour. He stopped and scratched his head when he didn't find any trace of the Stoners' wagons.

"Two wagons don't up and disappear into thin air," he said. His Appaloosa nickered softly, agreeing with him. "Where would I go if I were a pigheaded son of a bitch like Immanuel Stoner?"

Slocum climbed to the summit of a small rise and tried to figure out Stoner's route. In the darkness, he was well-nigh blind. Slocum stretched, yawned and knew there was no point going on until dawn. He made a campfire and fixed a can of beans and ate a bit of the moldy bread in his saddlebags. Then he stretched out and slept heavily until after sunrise.

With daylight bringing colors and detail into the valley, he saw a hint of a crossing canyon, maybe half the size of the one taken by Carter and the wagon train. Slocum made his way toward it and by noon found deep ruts left by a heavily-laden wagon. He smiled crookedly as he dropped to the ground to study the tracks.

"These are the Stoners' tracks. I'd bet a gold double eagle on it," Slocum said, running his fingers along the edges of the ruts to determine how far behind the errant sodbusters he might be. The imprint still carried a sharp edge, showing that he wasn't too distant.

Swinging into the saddle. Slocum kept the Appaloosa trotting until he reined back suddenly. The wagon tracks vanished, as if they'd never existed. Slocum had expected the ruts to change with the terrain and maybe he would even lose them for a spell as the wagons rolled over rocky stretches. But the tracks abruptly stopped in the middle of a grassy area.

"How'd they do that?" he wondered aloud. Slocum stared around, seeing that he had come quite a ways into the branching canyon. The walls were pulling in around him, but there wasn't any sign of a river that might give him problems, as in the other valley. The spring squalls wouldn't be as dangerous as a sodbuster able to vanish, as he had.

He rode on another mile and saw the tracks start up again as mysteriously as they had stopped. Curious, Slocum dismounted and knelt to study the spoor more carefully. He frowned when he saw the tracks up close. Using his hand as a ruler, he measured the width.

"Whatever made these tracks wasn't a prairie schooner," he told his attentive horse. "Too small. And come to think on it, there's only one wagon, not two." Slocum started away from the tracks and stared when he saw footprints. At least two men, maybe three, walked alongside the wagon.

"Might be a light wagon from the depth of the tracks, but it's not the Stoners'," he decided. Slocum started scouring the area for any indication of a settlement. Another twenty minutes riding brought him to an old road, long since overgrown by grass and weeds because of disuse. The road curled back in the direction he had come and stretched down the edge of the canyon and around a bluff jutting out sharply from the canyon walls.

Slocum shivered, feeling as if he were being watched. He always heeded such feelings. More than once they had kept him alive. But the canyon seemed deserted. Only the mournful howling of wind along the high canyon rim sounded. Even the few trees sprinkled along the canyon bottom seemed muted and free of wind moving through their long limbs.

If anything, the stillness was oppressive. Slocum checked his Colt Navy, making sure it carried a full six loads. He usually rode with the hammer resting on an empty cylinder to prevent accidental discharge. Somehow, he felt he might need the extra round very soon.

Slocum cut away from the old road and started scouting in earnest. Every sense came alive. He smelled the pollen in the air and saw faint movement as a sluggish breeze stirred a few aspen leaves, turning them into brightly rippling silver in the warm sunlight. But he couldn't shake the feeling of being watched.

His keen eyes scanned the upper canyon rim for any sign of a spy. Not a flash of sunlight off metal betrayed the hidden watcher, but Slocum knew the unseen snoop might be on the canyon floor, hidden in any of a dozen groves of trees he had passed. More than once Slocum doubled back to catch anyone on his trail. And he was always disappointed.

Just past midday, Slocum stopped to eat by a stream bubbling out of a crevice in the canyon wall and filling a small pond. Enough grass grew for his Appaloosa to enjoy a good meal, and Slocum wanted a solid rock cliff at his back as he ate. But he had hardly refilled his canteen and gotten some water to brew coffee when he went cold inside.

A single white-and-gray feather caught under a rock told him who the watchers must be.

His hand flashed for his six-shooter as he looked around. The sensation of being spied on didn't go away, but Slocum saw no sign of the Indians who had left the feather. He walked around the muddy area near the tiny pond and saw the scuff marks left by moccasins.

"Cheyenne," he decided, studying the eagle feather and the moccasin tracks. Slocum moved to put his back to the rock and waited for a flight of arrows that never came. He relaxed and decided the Indians had been here earlier, but not too much before him.

Eating jerky with a bit more of the stale bread and washing it down with water—he decided against a fire to brew coffee—Slocum thought hard on what he should do. Finding the Stoner party took on added urgency. Immanuel Stoner wasn't the kind who would go to ground and let a band of savages pass by unchallenged. His truculence would sure as hell get him scalped—and his wife Lottie and son and daughter. Slocum shuddered thinking of lovely Sarah's hair being separated from her head.

Then he shuddered even harder, knowing the Cheyennes weren't likely to kill her, as they would the rest of her family. She would be taken prisoner, unless luck favored her and she was killed in their initial attack.

Better dead than captive for such a lovely woman, Slocum decided. He gulped down the rest of his meal and quickly stashed everything in his saddlebags. Finding the Stoner family was more important than ever, and he wasn't even sure they had come down this canyon. The tracks didn't look to be theirs, but where else would they have gone?

Slocum couldn't imagine a stubborn man like Immanuel Stoner turning around and going back to Missouri. Admitting defeat, and for no good reason other than not wanting to ford a stream, wasn't in the man's character. Stoner and his family must have come this way, even if Slocum had missed their tracks.

And who had left the other tracks? The light freight wagon hadn't rumbled past more than a few hours ahead of Slocum. Three men had walked alongside, possibly heading for a town farther up the canyon. That worried Slocum more than a little, though. The road wasn't in good enough shape for a town with even a handful of people.

"Maybe they get their supplies from down the other end of the canyon," Slocum said to himself, eyeing the steep walls with some distaste. A sniper on the rim might put a bullet through him before he knew it. He had been a sniper during the war and had spent many an afternoon waiting for the flash of gold off a Union officer's braid. A shot, perhaps two, and the enemy company lost its field commander.

A sniper killing him would doom the Stoners, if they were even alive.

Slocum rode a tad faster and found more trace of a Cheyenne party.

Then he went cold inside because he saw something more than fresh spoor from the Indians. The Cheyenne's trail was laid down on top of freshly dug ruts made by two heavy wagons, one following the other. Slocum measured the width of the tracks with his hand and these were more than a foot wider than those he had discovered earlier.

"Well," he said slowly, trying to figure out his best course of action. "I reckon I found the Stoners. Seems that the Cheyenne have found them, too." Slocum walked along the trail for a hundred yards and discovered more evidence that the Indians followed the settlers and not the other way around.

Cursing his bad luck and knowing he might not be able to get Immanuel Stoner and his family out of the trap they'd worked themselves into, Slocum mounted and rode along at a trot. The canyon didn't carry sound like most he had seen. The utter silence wore heavily on his nerves and turned him jumpy. Though the wind rustled leaves in the sturdy oak and tall, thin, white-barked aspen, there was very little sound reaching him. It was as if somebody had sneaked up when he wasn't paying attention and stuffed cotton in his ears.

But Slocum knew better. If anything, he was keyed up and straining for any indication he was riding into a trap. The clop-clop of his horse's hooves convinced him he hadn't gone deaf and not noticed it. And from high up on the canyon rim came the faint but unmistakable whine of wind working its way through rock. It was just that little of the normal clutter of sounds carried far down on the canyon floor.

"Keep driving those wagons, Stoner," Slocum muttered. If the sodbuster slowed, the Cheyenne would overtake him. And they might have already. Slocum eyed the deep-blue sky, squinting into the sun. He didn't see any sign of buzzards wheeling about, hunting their noonday meal. That might be a good sign.

And then again, the carrion eaters might already be on the ground with their gory feast.

As sudden as a clap of thunder, Slocum heard the sharp snap of a whip, followed by the creaking of harness-leather and the rattle of wheels.

"Get up," he urged his Appaloosa, forcing the tired animal into a gallop. He thundered along the path already taken by the settlers and rounded the butte he had been angling toward all day. Slocum almost ran over Immanuel Stoner and his family.

"Mr. Slocum!" came a delighted cry from the back of the trailing wagon. "Here we are!" Sarah Stoner leaned out of the back and waved to him. He waved back and kept riding as hard as he could. They must not know the Indians were close or they would have sped up—or tried to form a defensive perimeter.

"Stoner!" Slocum called, panting harshly from the hard ride. "Cheyenne. You got a party of Indians trailing you!"

"What are you carryin' on about, man?" demanded Stoner from the driver's box. The man half-stood and peered around the flapping canvas cover at Slocum. "We're not goin' back to the wagon train. We're forging a path on our own. This way's got to be shorter."

"And we don't have to cross no damn river," chimed in David Stoner from the lead wagon. The younger Stoner put on the wagon's brake and pulled his rig to a halt, much to his father's annoyance.

"Git that wagon of ours movin', boy," the elder Stoner cried. "We don't have no time to waste with the likes of him." Immanuel Stoner glared at Slocum, as if he had been the reason they'd left the wagon train and set out on their own.

"I don't care if you're cutting out to find the Promised Land," Slocum said, pulling alongside the elder Stoner. "Carter wanted to know what happened to you and for me to see you back to the wagon train."

"I just said—"

Slocum didn't let the man finish his sentence.

"You got Cheyenne on your ass," Slocum said harshly. "If you don't do something about it, they're going to lift your scalps."

"Poppycock! There's no Indians in this valley. I never seen a finer spot than this. Why, we might find a decent place and stake our claim. Good, rich land and—"

Again, Immanuel Stoner was cut off in midsentence, but this time it was by a loud war whoop. A dozen Cheyenne braves painted for war came riding at them, war lances waving and rifles gleaming in the hot Wyoming sun.

3

"Father!" cried Sarah, coming from the rear of the wagon and pressing close. "We must fight!"

"Run for it," corrected Slocum. He slid his Colt Navy from its holster, glad he had loaded the sixth cylinder. He tried to remember if he had a full magazine in the Winchester riding by his leg. Slocum wasn't sure, but he reckoned he'd find out quick enough.

"We are no cowards. We will fight, as my daughter said," Immanuel Stoner declared, reaching for a Greener goose gun he had laid at his feet in the wagon's box. Such a weapon would be worthless unless the Cheyennes rode down his throat—and by then Stoner would have a dozen arrows buried in his chest.

"There must be a town up ahead," Slocum said, wheeling his Appaloosa around to face the advancing Cheyennes. "Go there, get help. Now!" Slocum's voice carried enough of a bark to it that Stoner stiffened and turned, as if he was going to obey.

Slocum saw that the other wagon carrying Stoner's wife Lottie and son David had already creaked and started down the canyon, heading for the nearby butte of wind-chewed soft red

21

rock. Slocum hoped there was a town around that outjutting. If there wasn't, the Indians would have at least three new scalps hanging at their belts before the sun set.

And two women for prisoners.

"Father, please, start driving. Do as he says. Mr. Slocum knows about these things and will come along." Sarah turned, her soft brown eyes on him carrying a combination of thanks and admiration Slocum wasn't likely to live up to. He waved them on and was relieved to see Stoner wasn't going to argue. Their wagon groaned as the oxen started pulling.

Slocum decided his rifle was the better weapon of defense. He shoved his six-shooter back into the cross-draw holster and pulled out the rifle. It was cold and hard and almost comforting in his grip.

His Appaloosa stopped after he fired the first round, but the Cheyennes reined back to assess the threat they faced. They must have thought they'd swoop down and kill two wagons filled with ignorant sodbusters. Now they weren't so sure they could do it without getting ventilated, and Slocum wanted to keep them guessing as long as possible to give Stoner the chance for escape.

He glanced over his shoulder and saw both wagons moving slowly—too slowly. But he couldn't expect a mustang's speed out of those heavily-laden wagons. The most Slocum could hope for was to draw attention from the town that must be ahead. The other tracks he had found, the ones with the men walking alongside, had to be a freight wagon heading to some unknown village. Even a half dozen more rifles would be enough to keep the Cheyennes at bay.

Slocum fired twice more and trailed after Stoner's wagons, knowing he had to find a place to make his stand. Firing from horseback prevented any accurate shooting. His Appaloosa began to shift and paw the ground nervously, upset at the loud reports from the Winchester.

"Get moving!" Slocum shouted after the retreating wagons, then hit the ground to drop behind a boulder that might give him some protection. Already war arrows arched up and came sailing down to stick in the ground not five yards away. It wouldn't be long before the Cheyennes found their range and filled the air with their deadly arrows.

Slocum rested his rifle on the boulder and squeezed off a shot. One Indian's pony stumbled under him, throwing the rider. The Cheyenne was unhurt, though. The Cheyenne came to his feet and waved his fist in Slocum's direction. It was too far yet to make out what the brave shouted as he turned and started for cover. Slocum tried to wing the running brave and missed twice. He cursed his bad luck. Killing an Indian's horse merited torture if they caught him. Like so many of the tribes, horses represented more than wealth to the Cheyenne. The animals were their lifeblood, their soul, what made them special in their society.

Slocum squeezed back for a third shot. The rifle's hammer fell on an empty chamber. Slocum drew his six-shooter and fired twice, more to keep the Cheyennes away than to hit them. He did a quick count and saw at least ten. He wasn't sure but there might be even more moving just out of sight in a thinly-forested area on the far side of the narrow canyon. If so, they were trying to circle and cut him off from any town deeper in the canyon.

Jumping onto his horse, Slocum rode hard, trying to reload his rifle as he rode. He fumbled and dropped a few cartridges, but this was a small price to pay for getting the Winchester ready for battle again. The brief fight had taken only a minute or two, but it had given Stoner a chance to get rolling at full speed. Slocum knew he would have to hold back the tide of Indians for several minutes to insure the settlers' escape.

He angled toward the butte and its craggy base. Slocum saw a dozen places he might make a good stand and finally found the perfect spot. He galloped hard for it, hearing the war whoops of the pursing Cheyennes getting closer and closer. Hitting the ground running, he pulled his horse to relative safety and then scrambled onto the rocks and fell belly down. From his vantage point, he commanded a good view of the canyon behind him.

Placing the box of cartridges to his left, Slocum began firing. He went through the rifle's magazine and reloaded, then emptied the rifle once more before the Cheyennes decided not to pursue a frontal attack. He had wounded one overly-aggressive brave and maybe even winged their war chief.

"Come on, try it," he muttered to himself. He had fewer than twenty rounds left, but one more attack would be right fine by him. And it came almost as his plans were forming.

He got off another fifteen rounds and used the last of his cartridges to fill the Winchester's magazine before slipping back along the rock and rushing to his horse. The Appaloosa eyed him apprehensively.

"We held them back for damned near ten minutes," Slocum said, swinging into the saddle. "It's time for us to save our own scalps." He laughed as he rode, amused at the notion of an Indian scalping a horse. He sobered as he wended his way through the tumble of rock at the base of the butte. Somehow the notion of some brave stealing this fine Appaloosa bothered Slocum more than the prospect of his scalp as a war trophy.

He broke out of the maze of rock and back onto the floor of the canyon, leaving the main body of Indians behind. He hoped it would be several minutes before they realized their quarry had fled—and the plan might have worked except for a pair of braves separated from the main war party.

Slocum emptied his rifle at them and killed one. The other fled, whooping and calling for the others. Slocum sheathed his rifle and knew it would be a deadly race. If there wasn't a town ahead with a powerful lot of rifles prepared to do battle with the Cheyennes, he and the Stoners were done for.

He bent low over his Appaloosa's neck and pressed the horse to as much speed as he could. He didn't want to kill the animal under him from galloping too long, but he had to put as much distance between him and the Indians as he could.

Glancing over his shoulder, he saw more than two dozens braves thundering after him. Slocum knew his luck had run out. He stayed low even as his horse's strength flagged and the Indians slowly narrowed the distance. Where the Stoner party had gone, he couldn't say. At this speed, he ought to have overtaken them.

With the lead brave less than fifty yards behind him, Slocum rounded the tall butte and headed into a grassy valley that spread out in a gentle downslope. Any hope for finding a place to make his stand vanished. He would have been better off fighting to the death back where he had thought to decoy the Indians with a few well-placed shots.

Every step his Appaloosa took caused it to tire that much more and soon the horse was struggling, its flanks lathered and its breathing labored. Slocum drew his six-shooter and turned to fire point-blank at the Indian who had almost overtaken him. Slocum blinked in surprise at the result of the single shot.

The brave reined back savagely. The Cheyenne's horse dug in its back feet as if working a steer and then veered off. Slocum tried to get off another shot, only to find that he was galloping along the grassy area alone. All the Cheyennes had stopped at the edge of the meadow and simply watched in utter silence.

Slocum slackened the pace a mite to give his horse a rest. By the time he had put a full mile between him and the Indians, he pulled the horse to a complete halt. The Appaloosa stood, shaking and exhausted. Slocum was puzzled that the Cheyenne hadn't followed. From his vantage, he tried to find them and couldn't. They had chased him to the point of capture, then mysteriously stopped.

"I don't understand what happened," Slocum told his horse, "but I'm not complaining. It's about time Lady Luck smiled on me." He knew he would have been dead by now if they had pressed their advantage. Slocum had killed one and wounded one or two others—but that was only enough to infuriate a war party.

Walking his horse until it cooled gave Slocum the chance to look at the ground. Where the Stoners had gone was as much a mystery as why the Indians had cut short their pursuit like they had. Then he saw ruts cut through the grass and knew he was on the right trail.

Or was he?

Slocum frowned as he bent over and looked at the furrows in the soft ground. The tracks were fresh but hadn't been made by any heavy Conestoga wagon. Slocum placed his boot on one rut and measured the distance to the next. This wasn't made by even a freight wagon.

"Buggy tracks," he decided. "And made not more 'n an hour back from the look of them." Slocum kept walking until he came to a rise, then stopped and stared.

The buggy had overturned and lay at the bottom of a shallow gully. Slocum hurried down the slope and hitched his horse to the buggy wheel slowly turning in the air. He looked around for signs of the driver and saw no trace—not exactly.

Slocum's fingers moved along the edge of the buggy seat and came away sticky with fresh blood. But what held his attention was the bleached horse's skeleton. It was still harnessed up to the rig. Slocum couldn't figure out what was going on. The horse had died years ago, yet the buggy had fresh blood on it. He spun in a full circle, hunting for the buggy's driver.

No one staggered along, dazed by the accident. And Slocum saw only his own tracks in the soft dirt around the buggy. The bottom of the gully was well grassed and the ruts from the buggy wheels ended abruptly, as he would have expected. But anyone thrown from the buggy would have left tracks, too.

Slocum didn't see any. He turned back to the buggy itself, and a bit of yellowed cloth caught his eye. Slocum tugged hard and a large piece tore off from where it had been caught under the buggy seat. He stared at it, not knowing what it was for a moment. Then he took off his Stetson and scratched his head in wonderment.

"A lady's handkerchief," he said. "Linen, from the look of it, and it's been out here for a long, long time." Sun and weather had turned the cloth yellow and brittle. Turning the piece over and holding it up to the sky, Slocum saw the monogram: LAK.

But he found himself dizzy with the contradictions. An old scrap of a cultured lady's linen handkerchief, fresh blood, the skeleton of a horse still in harness, tracks laid down not an hour earlier—and nobody in sight.

Slocum took a deep breath and then mounted his horse. He must have missed something that more careful examination would have brought to light. Now, his duty lay in finding the Stoners and getting them back to Carter's wagon train. How he was going to get past the Cheyenne war party baffled him, but he'd find a way. He had kept alive this long by finding just the right path. There had to be another.

Slocum got to the far side of the meadow and looked back. The overturned buggy was hidden from sight by the depression in which it lay, and nothing but green valley and tall, distant stone canyon walls met his eye. For a moment, he wondered if he had somehow missed a cutoff that the Stoners might have taken in their race to get away from the Indians. Then he saw a notch in the woods surrounding the meadow that might accommodate a road.

Slocum rode along the edge of the grove and came to the wide stretch opening in the thicket. A slow smile crossed his face as he saw the deep ruts left by heavy wagons. Even better, he saw tracks that showed where *two* wagons had passed recently. This had to be the Stoner party. They must have skirted the entire meadow, not wanting to expose themselves in the wide-open center, though their route must have been more difficult for the attempts to hide from the Indians, as they fled.

Riding in the middle of the deep furrows gave Slocum a sense of accomplishment but no well-being. Too many unexplained things had happened to make him comfortable in this peaceful valley. He wasn't keen on returning to the wagon train, but that seemed to be better than spending another hour in this valley.

The road he followed was old and poorly travelled, save by the Stoners. It meandered through the woods, preventing Slocum from seeing more than a hundred yards ahead at any time. But he began to grow uneasy as he rode, the feeling of being spied on, growing. Slocum tried doubling back on the track once, then decided he was wasting his time. The only spoor he saw was left by the Stoners and his own horse.

But he was downright jumpy by sunset. Slocum hadn't found the Stoner wagons, and he was sure someone spied on him. He dismounted and walked along, keeping the muddy ruts in view. When the angry, wordless shout echoed through the woods, Slocum jumped a foot.

His hand flashed to his Colt Navy and whipped it out when gunshots sounded. Slocum didn't know if someone was shooting at him, but he wasn't going to remain exposed in the middle of the road and find out.

He ducked under the low limb of a scrub oak and peered into the gathering dusk for any movement.

"I got you in my sights, you mangy varmint," came the cold words from behind him. Slocum had fallen into a trap any greenhorn could have avoided.

Slocum prepared to turn and shoot it out with his unseen assailant. He dropped into a crouch, spun fast, and his left hand came back to fan the hammer.

Slocum faced . . . no one.

4

Slocum's left hand paused over his Colt's hammer. He had meant to fan off several quick rounds, cause some confusion, then see what he faced. But there wasn't anybody standing behind him.

He straightened, thinking this might be a Cheyenne trick. Spinning around, he made sure no one took advantage of his confusion to sneak up behind him. As far as Slocum could tell, he was alone in the woods. Yet he had heard voices and was sure someone had called him out. Walking slowly into the setting sun, Slocum's eyes scanned the ground for signs of boot prints. The soft earth showed nothing.

He kept a sharp eye out and cocked his head to one side to listen for the voices. All he heard were the usual changeable winds that always seemed to kick up when the sun sank behind the distant mountains and the air cooled for the night. A heavy bank of lead-gray clouds moved over the distant peaks, promising more rain soon. Slocum began to get a mite jumpy when he didn't hear the voices again. He was sure someone had come up behind him—but nobody had been there when he had moved to face his adversary.

"Getting spooked," he grumbled to himself. "Those Cheyenne must be hot on my trail by now." But Slocum didn't see any sign that the Indians had rounded the red butte and come into the valley. For whatever reason, they had simply stopped chasing him at the edge of the meadow. As he thought on it, Slocum decided he was about due for a break. The only luck he'd had lately was all bad.

He poked around a bit more, hunting for whoever might have been arguing so loudly. Nothing he saw on the ground or among the trees showed any other traveller along this stretch of ground, save for the ruts left by the Stoners' wagons. Shaking his head, Slocum got to his Appaloosa and mounted. The horse seemed uneasy, but Slocum's hand on a heaving neck calmed the horse.

"We'd best find the Stoners before it gets much darker." He urged the skittish horse forward at a faster pace than he liked in the gathering gloom. He didn't want to admit how anxious he was to get out of this valley. By the time he reached the point of cursing Immanuel Stoner for being such a pigheaded fool, he spotted the flapping white canvas of a Conestoga.

He rode forward, suddenly wary that he might be riding into a trap. Everything was making him nervous, and Slocum didn't like it. He wasn't a jumpy person by nature, but the very air in the valley seemed to close in on him, weighing him down like a heavy, wet blanket, cutting off his breath.

"There you are, Slocum," came Stoner's gravelly voice. "We was a 'wonderin' what became of you."

"Had to stop the Cheyennes from scalping you," Slocum said querulously. He was in no mood to bandy words with the sodbuster. He dropped to the ground and walked forward, aware that Stoner held the long-barreled shotgun in both hands and looked as if he might decide to use it on him.

"We found this valley, and I intend to make it our new home. There's no need to go gallivantin' all the way off to Oregon. That was a pipe dream, mothin' more." Stoner stood with his feet spread wide enough to take a punch and clutched the shotgun so tightly that his knuckles turned white. Slocum wondered what was going on with the settler.

Stoner had been one of the loudest opponents of Benjamin Carter taking the Sublette Cutoff out of South Pass instead of taking the Lander Cutoff, which went straightaway to Fort Hall. Stoner had insisted on the shorter path, even if it meant greater hardship and rougher travel because it would get them to Oregon sooner.

Now the sodbuster was willing to chuck his dreams and put down stakes in some unnamed valley. Slocum took off his Stetson and scratched his head, puzzling over it.

"Carter will want more than my word that you're happy. You send your boy back with me and tell the wagon master what you just said to me. That'll satisfy him. Then David can come on back here."

"What? Risk my only son to those savages?" Immanuel Stoner's voice almost cracked from strain, and Slocum began to get an inkling of the trouble. Stoner had lived a peaceful life in Missouri growing whatever crops suited him best. Why he had grown restless was anyone's guess. Easy money, richer land, the lure of adventure—Slocum had heard it all a hundred times over. But when the Cheyenne braves shot a few arrows at him, the sodbuster's courage had fled.

Stoner would be the last to admit it, but he was as scared as any jackrabbit chased by a coyote intent on a quick supper.

"No need to make a quick decision on whether to rejoin the wagon train or stay here," Slocum said, giving the man breathing room. He knew better than to force a confrontation. Even the most frightened rat fought like a cavalry company if backed into a corner. "You might decide different when you get a chance to look over the situation."

"It's good land," Stoner maintained, still gripping the shotgun even harder, as if it might save him.

"Good land, but the water might not be what you'd like," Slocum said. "Oregon's got both the land and the water up there at The Dalles." Slocum started to put his Stetson back on when he saw Sarah Stoner. The brunette smiled brightly when she came around the corner of the wagon and spotted him.

"Why, good evening, Mr. Slocum. I thought I heard Father talking to someone." There was more than Slocum wanted to think on wrapped up in that smile. He saw the devil dancing in the young woman's warm, brown eyes and wished he could find out what thoughts ran through her mind.

"We're camping for the night. Mr. Slocum's made a good suggestion," Stoner said gruffly. "We'll look this valley over in the morning and decide if we stay. Now, you go on and get supper ready."

"Mama's fixing it," Sarah said. "I wanted to go down to that stream and wash clothes." She made a vague gesture out into the woods. Slocum strained to hear a brook gently bubbling along, maybe a hundred yards distant.

"Too dangerous."

"Not if Mr. Slocum accompanied me," Sarah said. "David's busy repairing harness—we're going nowhere until he finishes. And you have your own chores to tend to."

"Go on and get about your work, then," Stoner said, frowning. His forehead wrinkled and his thick eyebrows looked like dancing caterpillars, so great was his displeasure at his daughter's suggestion.

Before Slocum could speak, Sarah grabbed his arm and dragged him away. When they were a few paces from her father, Sarah said in a low voice, "Don't cross him, Mr. Slocum. Just come along and watch over me while I do our wash." Again came the impish smile and the look in Sarah's mahogany eyes that Slocum couldn't decipher.

He silently took a double armload of laundry and followed her into the woods. He walked slowly and listened hard for any sign that they weren't alone. Slocum heard Stoner and his son back at their camp and saw Mrs. Stoner working over a low campfire, stirring something fragrant in a stew pot. And of Indians or others, he saw no trace. They were alone and farther from camp than he'd guessed when he saw the brook.

"We're looking for a good place to wash," Sarah said too loudly, as if she intended for the words to carry back to her father. She grabbed his arm and guided him upstream until they were a good quarter mile from the wagons.

"This ought to be a good place," Slocum said, seeing a dark pool of still water. The stream ran fast around some rocks and formed this backwater. He dropped his load and looked around, to be sure they weren't being spied upon.

As he turned back, Slocum found Sarah pressing into the circle of his arms. She was tall, her face just a little below his. Her lips were slightly parted and the expression on her face was one Slocum had seen before.

"Are you sure about this?" he asked.

Sarah pressed even closer, her breasts flattening against his chest. He felt her hot breath and accelerating pulse as she clung to him. She licked her lips and whispered huskily, "I've never been more sure of anything, John."

Then she kissed him.

Or did he kiss her? Slocum wasn't quite sure, and it didn't matter much. He felt hot lips greedily seeking his. Slocum's hands fit perfectly into the small of the woman's back as he pulled her willing body even closer. When Sarah lifted one leg and tried to wrap it around his waist, things got complicated.

"Wait, wait, John," she panted. Sarah tossed her head back to get long strands of brunette hair from her eyes, then she started to work at his gunbelt. She dropped his cross-draw holster to the ground and began fumbling with his pants. As Sarah bent over, Slocum saw down the front of her blouse.

He felt himself getting harder at the sight of her soft, warm, white breasts barely held back by the fabric of her blouse. Reaching down, he unbuttoned the blouse and let those succulent mounds of flesh tumble into his palms. He squeezed gently and was rewarded with a soft moan of pure pleasure.

Then it was his turn to moan in delight as the woman's lips closed around the tip of his hard organ. He gasped when her fingers began prying his balls free from the confines of his pants, and then he knew he wasn't going to be able to keep going like this much longer.

He wanted more, lots more from Sarah Stoner.

His hands went under her arms and lifted her until she stood again. Their eyes locked as Slocum began lifting her skirts. He hoped there wasn't too much in the way of frilly feminine undergarments to get in the way. The instant his hands found firm thigh, he knew his luck was running high.

"Yes, John, go on. I want you so!" Sarah pressed closer to him.

"What would your pa say?"

"To hell with him!" Sarah raged unexpectedly. "He's such a tyrant. From the minute I saw you, I wanted for us to be like this. Together. And I don't care if he's been badmouthing you. I want you, John. And I know you want me. I can see it every time you look at me!"

Sarah hiked her skirts, and Slocum got a view of paradise. Once again the woman lifted a long, trim leg and hooked it around his waist. This time there wasn't any clothing to get in the way. Slocum felt his hard length slide along down-covered flesh, wetted by the juices leaking from within the woman's body.

He closed his eyes and tried to keep from coming like a young stud with his first woman when Sarah gripped his length and stroked vigorously. She guided him to the tight canyon he yearned to enter. For a moment, he paused when the head of his manhood found the damp entrance, then he lifted and surged deep into her interior. Stars spun wildly above him as he was surrounded by squeezing female flesh. Sarah groaned and twisted back and forth, passion seizing control of her.

Bending a little, Slocum began nibbling at Sarah's neck and earlobe and lips, even as his hands worked along the smooth curves of her breasts. His questing fingers found the taut buttons of her nipples. He squeezed down hard, and Sarah let out a shriek that carried a long ways in the silent night.

"Sarah, don't—" he started to warn her. The woman silenced him with her lips, hungrily kissing him as if she hadn't had a man in a blue moon.

And maybe she hadn't. It had been a spell since Slocum had found a woman this willing and even longer since he'd been with one so lovely. Moving up and down pulled him in and out of her clinging, tight tunnel. As Sarah twisted from side to side, this added a new thrill to their lovemaking.

Every thrust, every tweak on her nipples, and kiss on her neck pushed Sarah's desires higher until she was whimpering with abject lust—and it was a lust Slocum shared fully.

His entire length burned hotly as he stroked back and forth, stoking the fires of their mutual cravings. He felt her frenzied heart beating through her hard, copper-colored nipples and knew she was close to a climax by the warm flush rising on her snowy shoulders.

Arching his back, he drove upward even as Sarah tensed the leg she had snaked around his waist. This drove him to uncharted depths within her and lit the fuse buried within his loins. Slocum thought dynamite had exploded within his balls as he came.

Sarah clung hard to him, rocking and moaning as he spewed his seed into her. Slocum kept moving, driving hard and fast and then Sarah caught fire and erupted, just as he had. Her shriek rent the night and brought Slocum back to reality.

"Quiet!" He clamped his hand over her mouth, but the moment of intense ardor had passed. Sweating and limp, Sarah leaned against him. Slocum lowered her to the ground and knelt beside her.

She looked up, a look of complete adoration on her face. Then she burst out laughing.

"What's so funny?" Slocum demanded.

"Oh, nothing." Sarah giggled, then reached over and poked his flaccid organ. "This!" She laughed again, then moved around to throw her arms around his neck and give him a resounding kiss. "You're not like the other men I've known, John. You're different, better. A world better!"

She buried her face in his shoulder and for a moment Slocum thought she was going to sleep. Then he felt hot tears on his skin and knew she was crying. For a moment, he said nothing, wondering if he had done something wrong. Sarah pushed back and turned away.

"I'd better get started on the wash or Father will wonder what I've been doing."

She straightened her skirt and buttoned her white blouse, then began washing the clothing. Sarah kept her back to him but from the way her body shook, Slocum knew she was fighting hard to keep back a flood of tears.

"What's wrong?" he asked, feeling awkward. "Did I do something to offend you?"

"No, John, no! It's not you. It's my father. And—" Sarah bit back the explanation, wiped tears from her eyes and then got to scrubbing the clothes. "The reason we left Missouri to go to Oregon is partly me. I had a beau." Sarah swallowed and found the going hard.

"Your pa didn't cotton to him, so he upped and moved?" Slocum hardly believed that.

"Frank wasn't the kind of man to bring home to Sunday dinner, to meet your family," Sarah said. "He was wild, but he was going to settle down. We were going to settle down and—" Emotion seized her again.

"He was an outlaw?"

"Not really, but Father thought so."

This time Slocum said nothing. Being just a little bit of an outlaw was like a woman being a little bit pregnant. He suspected that Sarah put her boyfriend in the best possible light, just as Immanuel Stoner was likely to have thought the worst of him.

"I'll help. Don't want to take more time than your pa would think ordinary for this many clothes," Slocum said. He helped Sarah with the work, then hung out the clothing to dry in the soft breeze blowing across the valley. He sat and watched her in the light of the crescent moon rising in the east and wished they had time for another bout of lovemaking, this time slower, less driven by their rampaging desires and more by mutual exploration. Sarah Stoner was a woman Slocum wanted to know better.

"We can go back. The clothes'll dry anywhere," Sarah said suddenly, gathering the garments she had just hung out.

Slocum helped her, trying to put into words his chaotic thoughts. He finally asked, "What do you reckon your pa's going to do? Return to the wagon train or stay?"

"Can't rightly say," Sarah admitted. "When he gets a thought in his head, it scares him something fierce." She laughed, but this time without any humor. "He'll do whatever he wants."

"What does your ma think? And your brother?"

"They'll do whatever he says. They always do." Sarah walked briskly, Slocum trailing along. The night was getting colder around him.

And by sunrise it was positively chilly.

Slocum tended his horse before Immanuel Stoner rose, but he hadn't begun his breakfast when the man called out to him. Slocum walked over from where he had slept under a juniper, thinking most of the night about Sarah. He tried to keep his thoughts reined in when he stopped to talk to Stoner.

"We're going on into town," Stoner said, startling Slocum.

"What town?"

"And you call yourself a scout. Buzzard Flats, that's where," Stoner said scornfully. "We saw a sign back on the road yesterday. We'll see how friendly folks are in these here parts. Then I'll decide what we're going to do."

"Let's ride," Slocum said, seeing Sarah stirring inside the wagon. Her mother had slept next to her, and Slocum thought David Stoner might have stood guard, though he couldn't be sure. The boy's bleary-eyed gaze and occasional wide-mouthed yawn told of a sleepless night.

"We can be in town for breakfast," Stoner said, as if whipping up his courage. "Yes, sir, that'd be mighty nice. For weeks, I been hankerin' to get a good beefsteak instead of the maggoty food we've had so far."

Slocum rode ahead of the two wagons, eyes scanning the terrain for any sign of life. The entire valley seemed empty of life, save for a small bird or a curious rabbit sticking its head out to see what disturbed its burrow. Slocum worried that Buzzard Flats might be an outlaw town. This entire area of Wyoming was filled with outlaw hideouts. A family like the Stoners might find their welcome a bit strained.

Especially since Sarah was such a pretty woman. Men accustomed to killing to get what they wanted wouldn't think twice about plugging Immanuel Stoner and his boy, then having their way with daughter and wife. Slocum knew the killing would be terrible, if any owlhoot thought that was possible.

John Slocum wasn't the kind of man who'd simply give over a woman like Sarah.

"There, Slocum, see it?" called Stoner from his wagon. Slocum turned and saw a weathered signpost with the words BUZZARD FLATS painted in faded red. If he was any judge, that sign had been knocked over a year and more back. Nobody from the town seemed inclined to repair it. Or use the road.

This worried Slocum as much as anything else. The faint tracks in the muddy ground were old, almost ancient. No heavy freighters had come this way for a long, long time. How did the folks in Buzzard Flats get their supplies, if not by wagon through the canyon?

He knew there must be another way to the town, maybe from the other direction—but what lay to the north? As far as Slocum could recollect, nothing but miles of barren mountains lay in that direction. South Pass was the biggest town in the area, including Fort Bridger a ways to the south.

"Soda Springs, over in Idaho," he muttered to himself. "Might be that the town gets supplies from Soda Springs." But Slocum doubted this since it was a long, hard pull over steep mountain passes to the west. Better to bring supplies in from South Pass.

Slocum stopped his musing when he saw Buzzard Flats. Stoner called to his oxen and stomped down hard on his brake to bring his wagon to a halt. On the far side, David Stoner also came to a stop. They all stared at the town.

"Don't figure anybody's lived there in years," Slocum said. "That's a ghost town."

Most of the buildings were still standing, but only through the grace of long nails. Wood planks had rotted and the clapboard walls in several stores had holes big enough to ride through. Here and there a roof still arched over the building. Slocum smiled slowly when he saw that the saloon looked intact, as did the town jail. Some things were eternal.

Or seemed that way.

"Where'd all the people go?" asked Sarah from behind her father.

"Can't rightly say," answered Slocum. "This might have been a boomtown. When the ore played out, the miners left. All the merchants would follow them real quick like." He scanned the area and saw no trace of mine tailings or shafts. "Might have been something else," he concluded.

"You mean disease?" Sarah's eyes widened.

"I wouldn't get too upset over that prospect," Slocum told her. "This town's been empty for a long time. Anything that scared off the citizens would be gone with them."

"We can't know that," Stoner said, his voice carrying a hint of panic. "Might be cholera. That will race through a town and kill everyone within weeks."

"Pox," Slocum said callously. "Pox will do the same thing." He knew he shouldn't add fuel to the man's fears, but he wanted Stoner to return to the wagon train. Scaring the bejesus out of him might just be the way to do it. When Stoner feared some unknown disease more than he did the Indians that might be lurking at the mouth of the canyon, he'd be ready to catch up with Carter's train.

"You think so, Jo—Mr. Slocum?" said Sarah.

He shook his head so only she noticed. She smiled broadly at this joke on her father.

Before Slocum could say another word, a shot rang out. He sat straighter in the saddle, looking around for the source of the gunfire. The town seemed as deserted now as it had when he'd first set eyes upon it. And then came another shot, and another and another until a battle raged somewhere.

"You stay here. I'll find out what's going on." Slocum put his heels to the appaloosa's flanks and trotted forward, knowing he ought to wait for the gunmen to show themselves before riding into Buzzard Flats. But curiosity was getting the better of him. This town didn't have the appearance of a place where men lived—or hadn't recently.

Slocum knew he might find answers to questions that had been nagging him since riding into the valley.

Colt riding easy in its holster, Slocum slowed his horse to a walk. More gunfire sounded. He tried to find where it came from and couldn't. Echoes confused his sense of direction.

Then Slocum was diving off horseback, hitting the ground hard and rolling. A bullet had winged past his left ear close enough to take out a small, bloody notch. He yanked out his six-shooter and turned toward the saloon. That was the only building where a sniper might have gotten a clear shot at him.

Bent low, Slocum ran forward. He started to snap off a round or two but held back. He might need all six rounds when he found the unseen shooter. Two more bullets sought his body and missed, blowing away splinters from a post near his head.

He kept running, hit the rotted boardwalk outside the saloon and pressed his back against a rickety wall. Taking a deep breath, Slocum swung around, kicking the door off its rusty hinges. His Colt swung in an arc, looking for the man who had tried to bushwhack him.

Except for stringy, sticky cobwebs, the saloon was as empty as a gutted steer.

5

Slocum's trigger finger curled tighter, sure he had walked into a trap. Somebody was having a bit of fun before cutting him down, and Slocum wasn't going to let that happen. He stepped into the dusty, dim saloon interior and waited for more gunfire. Slocum's ears strained and heard only the settling of the floor under his feet as his unaccustomed weight made itself felt on rotting boards. The rising wind outside caused the decaying building to shift slightly, creating a groaning sound that was almost human.

But that wasn't what Slocum had heard. He knew gunfire when he heard it. And bullets had sailed past his head. Mistaking that was impossible. It had happened too many times for him to ever mistake it.

Slocum advanced slowly, his Colt Navy swinging from side to side, ready for action. He went to the dirty bar and cautiously peered over it. Nothing but dust and undisturbed debris lay behind the long pine board bar. The mirror once reflecting everything in the room had long since been shattered into a thousand shards. Anyone moving behind the bar would have ground the glass into the floor and noisily betrayed his presence.

He walked to the rear of the saloon and peered out the door. The hinges had long since given up any hope of holding the heavy door and had pulled free from the wall. Slocum gently nudged the door with his boot. It crashed to the floor. No one had passed this way recently.

Turning his attention to the stairs leading up to what must have been the the gin mill's cribs, Slocum studied the boards. Several were broken but all carried a heavy layer of dust. If anybody waited for him upstairs, they hadn't used these stairs to get there.

Frowning, Slocum returned to the front door and peered into the street. Weeds grew everywhere, urged to incredible height by the heavy rains and warm sunlight. Not having boot soles trampling them helped a bit, too, Slocum decided. Buzzard Flats was deserted as any ghost town he had ever seen.

Edging out, keeping his back to the saloon's front wall, he went to the side and looked down the alley. Then he walked to the other side of the saloon and spun around, gun leveled and ready for action. Again he found nothing but emptiness. Feeling a little foolish, Slocum holstered his six-shooter and went back into the street.

Patting his horse's neck, Slocum said in a low voice, "I swear those were bullets trying to take off my head." He reached up and his fingers came away bloody from the spot where one slug had almost killed him. His ear hurt more than if he'd stuck it in a campfire, but Slocum used this pain to force himself to caution again.

He *hadn't* imagined the bushwhacking.

Keen green eyes scanned the rows of deserted buildings and saw nothing. Shaking his head, Slocum mounted and rode slowly to the far end of Buzzard Flats. The town had never been large, maybe a couple hundred people in its heyday. Where had they gone?

Slocum turned his Appaloosa's face and trotted back down Buzzard Flats' main street and on out to where Immanuel Stoner and his family waited impatiently. Slocum saw Sarah's concerned look and tipped his Stetson in her direction, letting her know all was fine. He hoped he didn't look too bloody or he might frighten her unduly.

"What's going on?" demanded Stoner, jumping down from the wagon's box. "I heard gunshots, and you were gone a powerful long time."

"Can't say what's going on. The town might be deserted." Slocum winced as his hand brushed over his ear. He realized for the first time that most of the day had vanished while he poked about Buzzard Flats.

"You just shootin' off that fancy six-shooter of yours to spook us?" asked David Stoner. Slocum ignored the youth. He didn't have too high an opinion of him and saw no reason to waste time answering his idiot questions.

"There's no one there, as far as I can tell," Slocum said to Stoner. "But I might be wrong."

"Well, are there or aren't there people in Buzzard Flats?" Stoner turned truculent. His chin jutted out, making Slocum want to take a good poke at him. He held back.

"Didn't see anyone, but the Cheyenne are a sneaky bunch. That was a war party we ran afoul of back in the canyon. They might be playing their own game, having a bit of fun with us." Slocum had never heard of Cheyennes doing this. The Indians were more direct. They fought fiercely or they slipped away to fight another day. Seldom did they play cat and mouse with their enemies.

But nothing about this valley—and Buzzard Flats—felt right to Slocum. Tracks that had no business being there led to an old buggy with fresh blood on the seat. Freight wagons ought to be everywhere, from the look of the trail in canyon. But those tracks simply vanished. And the Cheyenne had pulled back from their attack when they had Slocum dead to rights.

They hadn't taken him when he was within their grasp. Why not? What had spooked them?

"You were hired to keep those savages from harmin' us," Stoner said angrily. "Are they waitin' there for us or not?"

"Benjamin Carter hired me to scout for the wagon train," Slocum said coldly. Stoner was pushing him to the limit of his tolerance. It would not be too hard simply to ride off and let the Stoner family fend for itself. "I don't work for you, and I'm not going to get a dozen arrows in my back for no good reason other than you wanting to ride into Buzzard Flats."

"Please, Mr. Slocum," came Sarah's soft voice. "Please don't leave us out here. We need you—"

"Be quiet, girl," snapped Stoner. "Slocum can do what he pleases. I say we're going into that town and see for ourselves if this is a good place to homestead." Stoner climbed into his wagon and caught up the reins to his team of oxen. Slocum knew the sodbuster wasn't going to listen to reason. It was up to him to decide whether to stay with the Stoners a while longer and protect Sarah from her father's stupidity or to just ride on.

A new course of action hit Slocum. Would Sarah go with him if he asked her to leave her family? He didn't know and wasn't sure he wanted to find out. They were attracted to each other, but was there anything else between them? Slocum knew Sarah might have turned to him because of the way her father had dragged her away from her boyfriend Frank back in Missouri.

Slocum snorted in contempt. If Frank had any feelings for Sarah, he would have followed her to the ends of the earth. That he had remained in Missouri showed less interest in her on his part than Sarah had for him.

"I'll stay till tomorrow, if that suits you," Slocum said. He stared past Immanuel Stoner at the man's daughter. A smile came to Sarah's lips, and Slocum knew he'd made the right decision. Whether he asked Sarah to abandon her family could be resolved later, when he had a chance to think on it a mite longer.

Slocum rode far to one side of Stoner's wagon. David Stoner's wagon trailed behind in the mud, wallowing like a bloated hog. Slocum wondered what they had piled into those wagons. He always marveled at the useless gewgaws sodbusters thought necessary to put down roots at a new spread. Seldom did he see one who travelled light and well.

The wagons rolled down the weed-overgrown main street and came to a halt in front of what might have been a hotel.

The second storey had long since collapsed onto the ground floor, but behind the ruined hotel was a stable that appeared to be in good shape. This must have been what attracted Stoner to the spot—that and the stable lay at the far end of town from the saloon. Immanuel Stoner had the look of a man considering a nip of whiskey now and then to be the work of the devil.

"Here's where we'll stay for a spell," Stoner said. He urged his team forward another few feet and pulled the wagon near the demolished hotel. He tied down the reins and jumped to the ground. David Stoner rattled past and stopped his wagon in the area just beyond. A few burned-down shacks lay beyond. Otherwise, the Stoners had stopped at the edge of Buzzard Flats farthest from where Slocum had first entered.

"You're welcome to stay for supper, Slocum," offered Stoner, "but there's no reason for you to stay past morning. I like what I see. This is rich land, and me and the family'll have a good farm here."

"Don't rush your decision," Slocum said, dismounting. He had farmed most of his life before the war and knew Stoner was right. The entire valley was lush. The growing season this high in the mountains would be short, but the bright sunlight and adequate rain compensated. Stoner could make a good living, save for the fact there wasn't any sign of another human this side of the Cheyennes.

Slocum hoped Immanuel Stoner had the good sense to know he couldn't make it a hundred miles from the nearest settlement. Supplies had to be fetched and time would come when a doctor was required. But Stoner might be considering other factors. He seemed determined to keep his only daughter away from bad influences, such as Frank back in Missouri. That made Slocum think all the harder on whether to ask Sarah to come with him when he left in the morning. She would wither and die out here, without any other human beings but her family.

Slocum went to chop wood while Lottie Stoner and her daughter fixed supper. Slocum didn't ask where David and his father went off to. He appreciated the time away from the men almost as much as he did the chance to be alone with Sarah.

"Here's enough wood to last you the night," he said, dropping his armload. His reward was Sarah's bright smile. The woman started to say something when her mother came bustling up, a worried expression turning her face into a wrinkled prune.

"What's wrong, Mama?" asked Sarah. She glanced back at Slocum, as if to reassure him that she wasn't ignoring him.

"I heard it again," Lottie Stoner said apprehensively. She pointed toward the pile of the hotel. "There's where it came from. I heard it."

"What's that, Mrs. Stoner?" asked Slocum. He slipped the leather thong off his six-shooter's hammer. Slocum's ear burned as hot as if he had just suffered the wound.

"Sarah told me she heard footsteps over there. I told her she was being a foolish child, but—"

"But you heard the sounds, too?" Slocum finished. He saw that Mrs. Stoner was upset that her husband had abandoned her to go exploring.

"Mr. Slocum can investigate the sounds, can't you, John?" Sarah bit her lower lip in anxiety when she realized she had used Slocum's first name in such a familiar way. Her mother was so perturbed she didn't notice the lapse of manners—or question what it might mean.

"Reckon so," Slocum said. "You ladies stay here. If you go poking around while I'm out there, I might mistake you for an intruder." He drew his six-gun and set off in the direction of the tumbledown hotel. They might have heard nothing more than a rat hunting for a meal in the piles of boards or the darkness could have confused them. Slocum smiled as he thought they could have heard Immanuel Stoner and his son rather than intruders.

He stopped at the edge of the hotel, staring into the twilight's shadows. The moon wouldn't be up for another hour and the darkness was almost complete. Rather than risking a broken ankle crossing the disintegrating hotel, Slocum circled the foundation. He kept his gun levelled, in case anything popped up. He heard nothing, but his sixth sense began to send messages of danger. Slocum turned more cautious as he pushed deeper into the ghost town.

After ten minutes, Slocum decided nothing would come of further search. He returned to the Stoners's camp, finding that David had returned.

"Where's your father?" Slocum asked the youth. David Stoner tensed, as if Slocum had struck him.

"Dunno," the younger Stoner muttered. "We was out there rootin' around, lookin' for something we might use. He wandered off and I don't know where he went." David Stoner crossed his arms and seemed to sink into himself fearfully.

"John," Sarah whispered. "I'm worried about him."

"He took the shotgun, didn't he?" Slocum didn't see the goose gun and figured Stoner had it with him. "He can use it. Even if he just fired it, we'd know where he was, if there was any trouble."

"Well, all right. If you say so." Sarah didn't sound confident, and Slocum wondered at his own motives. If he worried her enough, would she come with him? Or if he let her pa get into trouble he could never escape, might the young woman leave more willingly? Without Immanuel Stoner, the family would return to the wagon train and Slocum would rise that much higher in Sarah's estimation.

Slocum shrugged off second guessing his own motives. He thought highly of the lovely young brunette, but he would never see her father dead to further his own cause with her. Slocum was more of a man than that. Immanuel Stoner didn't frighten him. If Slocum intended doing anything with Sarah, he would do it openly.

That their assignation earlier had been hurried and hidden from the rest of the family was more out of consideration for Sarah's feelings than anything else, Slocum told himself. She had to decide how to deal with her blood kin.

"There," shouted Lottie Stoner. "I heard it again. Out there!" She pointed toward the middle of Buzzard Flats, where Slocum had searched. He hadn't even run across the woman's husband, much less a band of Cheyenne sneaking up on them. If the Indians wanted to ambush them, they'd sneak up and just do it. There was nothing to be gained by warning their quarry.

"What was it?" Slocum directed his question more toward Sarah than her mother. Sarah shook her head, her soft hair floating away from her head in a soft brown cloud. Slocum fought back the urge to go to her and kiss her hard. Just enough of the crescent moon poked above the trees to shine on her pale face. It turned Sarah into something angelic. He shook himself free of her spell when Lottie Stoner answered his question.

"Sounded like men laughing. A whole passel of them. Go find out what's happening, David." The woman's tone sounded exactly like her husband's as she barked out the command.

"He shouldn't go out alone," protested Sarah. But she moved closer to Slocum, obviously not wanting to be left alone when the men went poking about in the ruins.

"That's all right, Sarah. I won't be a minute." David hurried off into the darkness. For a few yards Slocum followed the youth's progress, then David Stoner turned behind a pile of wood and vanished. All that was left were the moonlight-filled footprints in the soft dirt.

"There's nothing to worry over," Slocum said. "There'd be something more happening if anyone wanted us dead."

"The Indians," protested Lottie Stoner. "You said so yourself. They might be out there and—" She cut off her diatribe when a scream cut through the still night.

Slocum's hand flashed to his six-shooter. He pushed Sarah back with his left hand as he moved in the direction her brother had taken. He couldn't identify the cry as coming from David's throat, but who else was out there?

"You both stay close to the fire," Slocum ordered. "Don't go off unless you're told to."

He didn't want them coming up behind him in the dark. He might shoot first and think about his target later. Slocum glanced at the women to be sure they were going to stay put, then ran off toward the last spot he'd seen David Stoner. Where Immanuel Stoner had gotten off to, Slocum didn't know or much care. Residents or not, Buzzard Flats wasn't the hospitable town Stoner thought it to be, and Slocum wanted nothing more than to be away from it.

Crouching low, Slocum moved around the pile of dilapidated walls and tumbled roofs from several stores. His nerves almost got the better of him when a rabbit burst out of the heap and raced into the darkness. Slocum calmed himself and kept moving, alert for a trap. The Cheyennes might let out a scream and then settle down to see who would answer the wordless call for aid.

But the Indians knew who they faced. They had chased settlers and a lone man into the valley. There wasn't any reason for them to be this cautions in their attack.

Slocum almost fell over the prone body. He stepped away, his six-shooter swinging down to cover the man stretched out on the ground. Then he recognized David Stoner and knelt beside him. Someone had slugged him from behind. Slocum's hand came away bloody from the deep cut. Vigilant, Slocum turned and hunted for David's assailant.

He saw nothing moving in the night, not even the rabbit he had chased off earlier. Slocum holstered his six-gun and struggled to get the youth over his shoulders. Staggering and slipping on the muddy ground, Slocum returned to the campfire where the two women rushed out to see what had happened.

"Is he hurt? Oh, David, my poor boy!" Lottie Stoner began tending her son before Slocum lowered him to the ground.

"How badly is he hurt, John?" asked Sarah. "He's not dead, is he?"

"There's a knot on the back of his head. He might have slipped in the mud and knocked himself out," Slocum said, not believing that for an instant. There hadn't been any footprints around David, but Slocum hadn't checked that carefully. And he didn't know how the youth could have hit himself on the head and ended up facedown on the ground. But he said nothing about it. David was already moaning as he came awake.

"What hit me?" were David Stoner's first words.

"You tell us," Slocum said, pushing the boy's mother aside. "Did someone sneak up on you? Did you see anybody?"

"No, nobody. I was just pokin' around that pile of old boards and don't remember nothin' after that." David Stoner rubbed his head and let out another groan far out of proportion to the wound. Slocum turned away in disgust.

"What's going on, John?" Sarah asked. "Who hit David?"

"Can't say. It might not have been such a good idea to spend the night in Buzzard Flats." Slocum spun, went into a crouch and had his six-shooter pointed into the shadows when he heard the soft sucking of a boot in the mud. Immanuel Stoner came into his sights.

Slocum let down the hammer on his Colt and straightened.

"What's going on here?" Stoner demanded. When he saw his son, he turned angry, thinking at first Slocum was responsible. Lottie Stoner explained to her husband what had befallen David. This did nothing to put Stoner in a better mood.

"You're supposed to be protectin' us, Slocum. Why'd you let some desperado do this?"

"I'm not your bodyguard," Slocum said. "I warned you not to come into this town. Something's wrong in Buzzard Flats, and I can't rightly say what it is. My advice to you is get away from here as fast as you can whip those oxen of yours."

"He did tell us not to come here," Sarah said, sticking up for Slocum.

"Hush your mouth, Sarah," cautioned Lottie Stoner. "You'll anger your father. We don't want that."

Sarah subsided but Slocum saw there was more than fear on Immanuel Stoner's deeply lined face. He was getting scared and was turning pale from fright. Slocum knew some folks weren't cut out to be pioneers. Stoner was one of them. He ought to have stayed on his nice, safe farmland in Missouri.

"Get everything into the wagons. We'll move on out of here, just as Slocum said." Stoner swallowed hard. "I didn't find anything here worth claimin' so we might as well move on," he said. Slocum knew he was lying. The notion of staking claim to this entire valley appealed greatly to Stoner, but the sight of his son with blood all over his head and his daughter and wife upset spooked him something fierce.

"Do you want to head back to the wagon train?" Slocum asked.

"Oregon's a fine place, from all accounts," Stoner said. "Might be a good idea to get back with Carter and the others."

"Yeah, a real good idea," Slocum said sourly. He saddled his Appaloosa and mounted. By the time he rode around, trying to scout a bit to see if he could find any trace of whoever had clubbed David Stoner, the wagons were ready to roll.

"Right on back through town and toward the canyon," Slocum called to them. David sat beside his mother, but the woman held the reins. Immanuel Stoner snapped the reins so hard the traces whipped into the oxen's sides. They started pulling, and Slocum was glad to be out of Buzzard Flats.

He rode slowly, wanting to put as many miles behind him as possible before dawn. They might rest a spell then and finally push on after he'd scouted out the narrow canyon where the Cheyenne had attacked them earlier. Slocum thought the Indians would have moved on. If the cavalry pursued them, they wouldn't stay in one place too long. With luck, he could get the Stoners back into line with the wagon train in a few days.

Even as this pleasant thought fluttered across his mind, Slocum heard a sound that reminded him of cannonade. He whirled in the saddle and saw Immanuel Stoner's wagon tipping precariously to one side. The back axle had broken, spilling Stoner, his daughter and the wagon's contents all over the muddy street.

6

"Anybody hurt?" Slocum shouted back. He saw Immanuel Stoner struggling to brush the dirt off his clothing and, to Slocum's relief, Sarah Stoner pushed out from under the tumble of her family's belongings to sit on the nearby rotting boardwalk. She rested her chin in her hands and sobbed openly. Slocum rode closer to see what he could do to calm the pretty woman.

"We'll never get out of this dreadful place," Sarah said fretfully, wiping at the tears leaving dirty tracks on her cheeks and trying to keep the tangles of her brunette hair from her face. "We should never have left home."

"Hush up, now," ordered her father. He stood beside his broken-down wagon, hands on his hips and looking as if he wanted to chew nails and spit tacks. "You're the goldarned reason we left a perfectly good farm in Missouri. You ought to have the good sense to know everything this family has done is for you."

Slocum started to speak, then clamped his mouth shut tight. It wasn't his place to come between father and daughter while Stoner was just blowing steam. From the way the sodbuster clenched and unclenched his fists, though, he wanted to strike out. Slocum wouldn't let him hit Sarah, and this quiet determination seemed to settle down the angry man when he saw the set to Slocum's jaw.

"Help me get the wagon unloaded so's we can see how bad the damage is." Stoner waved to his son to come over, also. David Stoner joined his father and Slocum in heaving the crates in the wagon-bed out onto the muddy byway. It took the better part of a half hour to get all the boxes unloaded with no attempt made to stack them. Slocum went to sit beside Sarah when he finished and Immanuel Stoner prepared to wiggle under the wagon to study the broken axle.

"We'll never get out of Buzzard Flats alive," Sarah said in a troubled tone. "I get this feeling in my bones. It's comin' on strong now, John. We're all gonna die here!"

Slocum put his arm around the woman's quaking shoulders to comfort her and found himself facing an irate Immanuel Stoner.

"Git your filthy hands off her, you no good drifter. I don't want your kind pawin' at my daughter."

"She's shook up pretty bad," Slocum said, taking his arm away, wondering if this was where he had to fight it out with Stoner. His son moved beside him, shotgun in his shaking hands. From the way David Stoner held the weapon, he was using it for a crutch to his courage. Slocum knew that made the youth even more dangerous. He might start firing without any idea what he was aiming at.

"She's my daughter. I'll do any consolin' that has to be done. Now you get your ass over there and help get the wagon propped up so we—" Stoner stopped when he saw the look on Slocum's face. To the sodbuster's credit, he knew death when he saw it.

"That's your wagon," Slocum said coldly. "You can fix it up or not. I'd as soon you dumped all this worthless baggage and rode in just one wagon."

"David, get to work," Stoner said, again frightened. Slocum pitied the man, even as he backed away from a fight he could never win. Immanuel Stoner went through life either running away or fearing everyone and everything. That wasn't a fit way for a man to live.

Especially one with a daughter as lovely as Sarah.

The two men struggled to jack up the wagon and get a rock under the broken axle. Slocum stood back and watched. If Stoner had been more civil, Slocum would have lent a hand. From his vantage, Slocum knew this axle was beyond fixing. They'd have to fashion a new one, and that meant at least a day's work, possibly two. He didn't know how handy Immanuel Stoner was at woodworking but he guessed David wasn't too good.

"We got to replace it," Stoner said, stating the obvious. "Do you reckon there's one left somewhere in town? Most of the buildings look to be intact. We might try the livery and see if an axle got left behind."

"Wouldn't do you any good, even if there was," Slocum pointed out. "The wood'd be rotted by now, just like the rest of Buzzard Flats."

"We don't have time to cut down a tree, shape the wood and season it. What are we going to do?"

"Don't worry about seasoning it," Slocum suggested. "When you get back to the wagon train, there's got to be someone with a replacement. I seem to remember people buying up all the spare axles in South Pass City."

"That Dickenson fellow," cried David Stoner. "The skinny guy with the big red nose. I know he got one back down the trail, just like Slocum said. What's he need a spare for? His load's not anywhere near as big as ours."

"Just last a few days on a green wood axle, that's all you need to do," said Slocum. "You'd better get some sleep and start hunting for a likely tree in the morning."

"There must be something in this good-for-nothing town we can use," protested Immanuel Stoner. "We'll look real hard before we go choppin' down a tree."

"Suit yourself," said Slocum. He took a deep whiff of the night air and turned his face to the sky. Heavy clouds from the mountains slipped across the sliver of moon and hid it. The distinctive odor of rain hit him like a slap. "You'd better get under cover. The sky's fixing to open up and drench us again."

"Can't see it," protested Stoner. "I been a farmer all my life, and I know when rain's gonna come." Stoner stopped talking when a heavy, cold raindrop hit him in the face. Slocum refrained from commenting. If Stoner wasn't any better a farmer than he was a weatherman, only luck had kept him and his family from starving.

"I'm going to see how much protection yonder saloon affords me," said Slocum. "You'd all be advised to join me. It'll be a sight drier there."

"We'll camp under our wagons," Stoner said, as stiff-necked and obstinate as ever.

"Have it your way," said Slocum, dismounting and going to the saloon. He doubted the roof was intact after all the neglect, but down in the main salon would still be drier than any place he could find out in the open.

He led his horse into the saloon and began unpacking his saddlebags when a bolt of lightning split the sky. For a moment it was brighter than day outside. Slocum blinked, thinking he saw a tall, bedslat-thin man with arms crossed over his chest standing on the far side of the street, watching him intently. When a second lightning bolt lit up Buzzard Flats, the man had vanished, and Slocum wasn't sure just what he'd seen.

Shaking it off, he spread his bedroll and lay down. He had just drifted off to sleep when he heard the planking near the door creak once. Slocum's eyes shot open, and he reached for his six-shooter. He hesitated to cock it, afraid he might scare off his nocturnal visitor. Waiting proved a good thing.

He saw a silhouette in the saloon's open door—and Sarah Stoner slipped into the room.

"John? Are you awake?" she called softly.

He pushed his Colt back into its holster. "I'm over here, by the bar," he said in a low voice.

"Good. I couldn't spend another second out there in the rain. I was gettin' wet and I couldn't sleep and—"

And Sarah snuggled under Slocum's blanket. His arm went around her, as natural as could be, and in a few minutes he found himself holding the sleeping woman. Her warm breath gusted across his chest. Slocum lay back and stared up into the darkness, wondering what he was getting himself into. If Sarah's father found her like this, there'd be hell to pay.

Slocum shrugged it off. He could think of worse reasons to get into a squabble.

Just before daybreak Slocum stirred and noticed the empty spot next to him under the blanket. Sometime during the night Sarah had left and returned to her wet bed under the family's wagon. Slocum stretched like a cat and decided Sarah had good sense. He wasn't ready to face down her father, and he reckoned neither was she.

Slocum rolled his blanket and stowed his gear in the saddlebags, then brushed down the Appaloosa. The horse stomped and pawed at the boards under its hooves as Slocum worked, but this nervousness came from hunger rather than fright.

"There, there," Slocum soothed, finishing his grooming. "We'll ride out a way and find you some fresh grass. It surely does look sweet in the valley." The horse accepted this and settled down, letting Slocum lead it from the saloon into the open air.

The rains had left behind tiny seas and an ocean of mud, but Slocum hardly noticed. The slowly lightening sky was clear as a bell, the last traces of stars slowly vanishing as the sun poked above the distant rim of mountains. He sucked in a deep breath of fresh air and knew why he preferred the trail to the city. No town, be it San Francisco, New Orleans, or St. Louis came close to giving him the exhilaration he felt now.

Slocum knelt and looked under the wagon and saw Immanuel Stoner and his son all caked in mud. They had been too pigheaded to come indoors while it was raining and now were badly in need of a bath neither was likely to want. Lottie Stoner had slept inside the other wagon, and Sarah was already working on breakfast. She smiled brightly and waved to Slocum, then went back to her work when she saw her father bustling about their camp.

"Glad you decided not to sleep away the day, Slocum. We got work findin' a tree and cuttin' it just right. We need to shape it for the axle, then get on out of here. Think we can do it in a day?"

"We can, if you're good enough a carpenter," Slocum said. "I'm going to range out and see if I can find where the Cheyenne got off to. By the time I get back, you ought to have the axle repaired."

"But—" Stoner sputtered and tried to correct what he saw as a mistake on Slocum's part. Slocum tipped his hat to Mrs. Stoner and Sarah, then swung into the saddle. Getting away from the sodbusters would do more for his disposition than breaking bread with them. Stoner had thought to get Slocum to do his work. Slocum had other ideas.

There was too much about Buzzard Flats that puzzled Slocum. He wanted answers and wasn't likely to get them if he stayed too close to the Stoners. He would get too caught up in their family squabbling.

Riding hard for ten minutes, Slocum slowed to a walk and then dismounted to let the Appaloosa rest. He fumbled in his saddlebags for some jerky. It wasn't as good as he'd have gotten from Sarah, and the company was nowhere as pretty, but Slocum didn't mind. He let the horse graze on a large patch of grass as he started exploring on foot.

The rain had left puddles everywhere and erased any tracks left by whoever had bushwhacked him the day before and then slugged David Stoner. But Slocum's eyebrows rose as he saw fresh buggy tracks angling off toward the canyon.

He got down on hands and knees and studied them, growing more baffled by the minute. These looked to be identical to the tracks he had seen before that led to the overturned buggy. The left wheel had wobbled a mite and Slocum found evidence of it in the tracks. But that couldn't be. The buggy was ruined and abandoned in the canyon.

More perplexing, someone had ridden damned close to Buzzard Flats after the rain had stopped. Where had they come from—and where were they going?

Slocum tried to make a guess as to direction of travel. He had assumed the tracks were leading from the town, but he might be wrong. He hadn't seen any track closer to Buzzard Flats, so assumed the buggy was leaving. And he surely hadn't come across any such carriage along the road.

"Looks like we're going back into the canyon, want to or not," he told his Appaloosa. The horse neighed sullenly, not wanting to leave its meal. Slocum let the horse graze a few more minutes before mounting and riding alongside the buggy tracks. They were deep and so distinct a blind man could follow them.

Or so Slocum thought. In the middle of a field, the tracks suddenly stopped. Slocum thought the buggy might have rolled over a rocky section of ground but examination showed it to be as muddy and soft as the ground holding the fresh tracks. He examined the spot where the ruts ended and couldn't figure out what had happened. It was as if a giant eagle had swooped down from the sky, lifted the buggy from the ground, and carried it off.

Slocum had seen some mighty big birds in his day but none that large.

"What happened to the horse pulling the buggy?" he asked himself. The buggy might have been swallowed up by the very ground, but had the horse gone willingly, too? He took off his Stetson and scratched his head. Slowly turning in a full circle, he searched the terrain for any signs he might have missed. The tracks abruptly stopped and that was that.

Curious, Slocum started walking in the direction the buggy had been travelling. A stand of scrub oaks and junipers ahead might offer a solution to what seemed a question without an obvious answer. Before Slocum had gone halfway, he started getting the uneasy feeling of being watched. He had felt it before in the valley, and it came back stronger than ever.

"Let's make better time," Slocum said to the Appaloosa, swinging into the saddle. In the center of the field he was exposed. The trees offered better cover for him to see if anyone was pursuing him. He hadn't ridden more than ten yards when a shot echoed across the field. Slocum didn't know where the bullet went, and he didn't want to wait around to find out where a second round might go.

Spurring his horse, he raced for the trees. More shots followed him, one kicking up a spray of mud and water not a foot to his left. This gave him the incentive needed to keep the Appaloosa running at full gallop until they reached the sheltering trees. Slocum slowed the horse, then began circling to the left, hoping to catch sight of whoever tried to backshoot him.

Slocum stood behind a juniper and waited, watching carefully for any sign of the bushwhacker. It took almost a minute before Slocum saw the glint of sunlight off a rifle barrel across the field. The backshooter had hidden to the left of Slocum's line of travel and had tried to hit him from the side. Slocum had thought the man was behind, making impossibly long shots.

"Let's see how good you are," Slocum said softly, pulling his Winchester from the saddle scabbard. He levered in a round and began working around to get a shot at the bushwhacker. It took better than ten minutes. Slocum was in no hurry, and he wanted to make the sniper begin to get antsy. He had learned patience during the war, and it always paid off.

Always. Slocum crouched behind a mound of decaying vegetation and peered over the top. Not ten yards away a burly man dressed entirely in black anxiously searched for him. Slocum raised the rifle to squeeze off a killing shot, then stopped.

The man had answers to a whole passel of questions Slocum wanted answered. Slocum lowered the rifle and melted back into the woods, moving to get behind the backshooter. He blinked in surprise when he found the man's horse— and more.

Three horses were tethered and straining at their bridles to get to the lush grass growing at their hooves. Slocum moved into a shadow and wondered where the other two riders might be. He was sure only the one bushwhacker had been shooting at him. From the appearance of the horses, though, the killer had two partners.

Slocum didn't cotton much to doing it, but he couldn't figure any other way of flushing the trio out of hiding. He lifted the rifle to shoot the horses. Just as he fired, a fusillade of lead crashed around him. Either he had betrayed his position or his luck had turned for the worse again. Whatever had happened, Slocum was driven to the ground and his shot went wild.

The horses reared and pawed at the air, trying to break free. They seemed barely saddle-broke—or maybe they were all stolen and not used to their new riders. Slocum didn't have time to think on the matter. He was too busy scrambling to stay alive. Lead kicked up dirt all around him and blew splinters off the fragrant junipers, bathing him in sticky sap.

Slocum crawled along the ground until he got deeper into the woods, then stood and cursed his bad luck. He ought to have plugged the first bushwhacker when he had the chance. Now he faced three of them, and he didn't know where they were. The only way out was to fight a bit smarter.

Slocum shinnied up a fir tree and settled down in a sharp vee formed by a sturdy limb and the trunk. His field of vision was limited, but he didn't think that would matter. One or two good shots would go a long way toward evening the odds against him. Then he would get his answers.

The crunch of boots on wet pine needles alerted him. Slocum raised his rifle to get off the first shot—and then heard the whine of a bullet. He fell hard to the ground, stunned and thrashing around like a fish out of water.

7

"I got the son of a bitch!" came the delighted shout from Slocum's right. Dazed, he couldn't do more than roll onto his side. Fire raced up his chest and exploded in his brain. Slocum sucked in a deep breath and winced as waves of new pain hit him like a sledgehammer. He didn't think he'd busted up any ribs, but it hardly mattered if he couldn't get away to lick his wounds.

A broken rib might heal itself. A bullet through his heart would not. Slocum flopped onto his belly and fired his rifle, not caring if anyone stood in front of the muzzle. He had to keep the bushwhackers at bay until he regained his senses.

They weren't too obliging. He heard heavy footfalls running toward him. Then the air filled with lead. Bits of vegetation from the forest floor kicked up around him as deadly bullets sang and whined through the woods. Slocum scrambled and got his feet under him somehow, then lunged forward to lie behind a fallen tree. The log gave him scant protection as two slugs ripped through the rotted wood and sprayed him with debris.

"Where'd he go? He can't jist up and vanish on us. I want his scalp!"

62 JAKE LOGAN

In spite of the claim, the man wasn't an Indian. Slocum jacked another round into his Winchester's chamber and swung the barrel around, waiting for the man to show himself. For the briefest instant, Slocum saw the red and white of a bandanna and used this as his target. He shot and knew right away that he hadn't even winged the bushwhacker.

"Here he is, Jeb. I got him run to ground over here. Come on over and help me!"

Slocum began firing at the sound of the man's voice, not sure where his target really was. For a brief instant, Slocum thought he might have hit his assailant. Then a new rain of lead drove Slocum back behind the decaying log.

"We got him now. He ain't gonna go nowhere but straight to hell!"

Slocum rolled onto his back and stared in the direction of that new voice. It might have been the man named Jeb the other bushwhacker had called on for assistance. Slocum knew the names of the men killing him didn't amount to a hill of beans. If they shot him, he'd be buzzard bait no matter what they called themselves.

Slocum got off another round and then began crawling along the length of the log, hoping to get out of the crossfire. With one gunman in front and another behind, he didn't have a Chinaman's chance of getting away alive unless he did something quick.

More hot lead sought his body, and Slocum realized the third bushwhacker was cutting off any possible retreat. He had to reduce the odds or he was a dead man. Sticking his head up for a moment, Slocum drew fire and located the first gunman. A single shot kept the gunman pinned down—and emptied the Winchester. Slocum had only the six rounds in his Colt Navy keeping him from feeding the worms.

He took a deep breath and pushed the pain in his side away. Slocum drew the six-shooter and got ready to make a run for it. As long as he stayed behind the log he was a sitting duck.

Two shots at the gunman sneaking up behind him forced that backshooter to take cover. Slocum got his feet under him, intending to make a headlong charge in that direction.

He might overwhelm one man. All he had to do was keep from getting shot in the back while he did it.

Surging, Slocum rushed forward, ready to fire if the gunman showed his face. He felt rather than saw guns being trained on him—and then he heard the report of another gun, this one of smaller caliber. Slocum fired into a bush where he thought one bushwhacker hid and was rewarded with a startled yelp. He knew he hadn't hurt the man badly, but he'd scared him enough to ruin his aim.

Slocum shot past, his six-shooter empty now. It rankled that he had to run like a rabbit to save himself, but there was no other way out of the trap. He had fired every round in both six-gun and rifle. There wasn't any way he could tangle with three armed men and hope to come out alive.

Panting from the hard run, Slocum heard more gunfire behind him. The lighter pistol cracked twice more and was answered with the deeper roar of the bushwhackers' guns. Whoever had blundered into the forest had saved Slocum's life. Slocum wished he could take the time to thank his unseen rescuer but getting back to his Appaloosa and the saddlebags hanging behind the saddle was more important.

He sucked in all the air he could, wincing in pain as his injured ribs grated in his chest. Slocum threw open the saddlebags and pulled out his spare Colt Navy. Then he fumbled out two loaded cylinders, knocked out the empty one in the six-shooter resting at his hip and got it ready for a decent fight.

Slocum whirled about, ready to go back into the dense woods and give supporting fire to his rescuer. He paused and listened hard. His ears rang from the previous gunfire—but he didn't think it was possible to miss new discharges. The fight in the forest was over.

Slocum considered what had to be done. He might bungle into the woods and get himself ambushed again, or he could ride back to Buzzard Flats and build a fire under the Stoner family to get them out of this valley. He hated the idea of leaving his Winchester behind that rotting log, but he knew he didn't have much choice.

64   JAKE LOGAN

Either his rescuer had been cut down or he had gotten away. Slocum doubted the bushwhackers were inclined to take prisoners. He wanted to thank whoever had saved his hide, but that would have to wait a while. Or maybe forever.

Slocum mounted and turned his Appaloosa toward Buzzard Flats. He had intended to scout the canyon for Indians. That menace seemed too distant to matter now that he had found the trio of backshooters.

He rode only a few dozen yards when his sense of duty got the better of him. What if the bushwhackers had wounded the man who had laid down the fire allowing him to escape? The sharp crack of the small caliber gun told him that his savior didn't have the stopping power of the men he faced.

Slocum cursed himself and turned back for the woods. He hit the ground and drew both six-shooters, ready to help the man who had already helped him. The woods were cool and dark, heavy limbs blocking easy vision. Slocum circled and came back to the spot where the three horses had been tethered. He let out pent-up air when he saw the animals were long gone.

Dropping to one knee, he studied the ground. Three men had run back, mounted and then hightailed it. Slocum had misjudged the surprise element when his unseen deliverer had started firing. One man had routed three.

Slocum knew better than to stay in one spot too long. He didn't know why he had been saved, or if the unseen gunman had intended that. There might have been a falling out among bushwhackers, a fourth owlhoot wanting to kill three former partners. If so, Slocum was in as much danger now as before.

He made his way into the woods and tried to reconstruct what had happened around the tree where he had been shot down. A bullet had struck the limb and dislodged him. But no matter how hard he searched, Slocum couldn't find where the fourth man had entered the fray. Spoor from the three who had put him into their deadly crossfire was apparent everywhere. Slocum found spent brass and deep footprints. All three men had huge feet, one with a

GHOST TOWN 65

deep notch cut in his left bootheel and the other two with worn soles.

The fourth man might have just drifted on the wind for all the evidence of his presence that Slocum could find. From all the strange trails Slocum had found in the canyon and valley, he was past being surprised at anything about Buzzard Flats. He gave up the search and retrieved his Winchester from behind the log. He felt better having the long gun back. He felt even better when he got the last box of cartridges from his saddlebags and reloaded the rifle.

Slocum forced the Appaloosa to a brisk pace returning to Buzzard Flats and the Stoners. He had delayed too long in his search for the bushwhackers and the man who had rescued him. Duty called louder from the direction of the sodbusters than it ever could from some unknown gunman.

The overgrown road turned and went straight into Buzzard Flats. Slocum reined back hard when he saw that Immanuel Stoner and his boy weren't at their wagon. Slocum saw two felled trees and knew the the Stoners had been working to replace the axle. How well they had done on that job, he couldn't say.

And he wasn't about to ride over to the wagon to look. Buzzard Flats spooked him something fierce, and he couldn't say why. Strange noises in the night were to be expected in a town abandoned for years. David might have slipped and hit his head through clumsiness, and the other sounds the Stoners had heard could be discounted.

Slocum reached up and touched his ear where a bullet had creased it. There wasn't any more mystery where that slug had come from. He had met the three hombres responsible out near the mouth of the canyon, and they had tried to cut him down a second time.

"Get them on out of there, Jeb," came a gravelly voice Slocum recognized. He guided his horse to the burned out shell of a house and dropped to the ground. Soothing his horse for a moment, Slocum waited for an answer.

"Aw, Mark, why cain't we just do 'em here? I don't want to play your dumbass games."

"Who you callin' a dumb ass, boy? Get them on out here right *now*."

Slocum peered around the corner of the house and over toward the Stoners' wagon. He saw one man's broad back. A red and white bandanna hung around his bull-like neck, marking him as one of the bushwhackers. And the other one coming out of the saloon made Slocum reach for his Colt. He recognized the man as Marcus Tennyson. And it was no revelation when the man with the bandanna turned around.

"Jeb Tennyson," whispered Slocum. His fingers tensed on the butt of his six-shooter. He had run afoul of the Tennyson brothers two years back. He had been ramrod on a cattle drive up the Montana Trail. The Tennyson brothers had rustled half the herd outside Lusk and stampeded the other half over a cliff.

"Will you two cayuses stop the bickering?" The third man came out, one hand on the back of Lottie Stoner's neck and the other holding a six-shooter. "You got no call to fight. Enjoy yourself. I intend to. This here filly's a fine one. Definitely to my liking." He bent and wetly kissed Mrs. Stoner.

The woman tried to get away, but the man's grip on her neck was too tight.

"Why do you want anything from her, Ethan?" asked Jeb Tennyson. "The young girl's more my style."

Slocum slipped his Colt from the holster as he judged distances and the chance of killing all three. He knew the Tennyson brothers, and he figured the third one was Ethan Crain, their cousin. Slocum had never crossed paths with the Tennysons' cousin, but he doubted Crain was any less an outlaw or cowardly backshooter than the others in his family.

But it was Jeb Tennyson who commanded his attention. If that yahoo wanted to harm Sarah, he'd find himself ventilated before he laid a finger on her.

Slocum lifted his Colt and aimed, only to have Jeb move out of view. The outlaw went to the rear of the wagon and caused a ruckus as he pulled Immanuel Stoner from the wagon bed. Slocum thought the Stoners must have repaired their axle but hadn't reloaded their belongings. They would have been better off leaving that wagon and departing, Slocum knew.

He couldn't spend any time crying over spilled milk. The Stoners had stayed, and now they needed rescuing. Slocum paused, considering what he might accomplish. The fourth man in the forest had saved him. Where had he gone after chasing off the Tennyson clan? Slocum didn't want to get mixed up with him when the outlaws were the real target.

Shrugging off the unknown rescuer, Slocum grabbed his rifle and ducked down an alley leading behind several of the dilapidated stores near the Stoner wagon. He wanted as good a shot as he could get. One killing shot, then another and chasing down the third owlhoot was only a matter of patience.

But the first shot had to be deadly.

"Listen to her howl, Mark. She likes me, I tell you." Ethan Crain shoved Lottie Stoner to the ground. The woman stayed on hand and knees. Her dress had been torn, and a wild, trapped animal expression marred her handsome face. Slocum knew she might erupt and be hurt for doing it.

Before Mrs. Stoner could get up, Jeb Tennyson kicked her hard in the belly. She grunted and collapsed, mewling like a stepped-on kitten.

"Go on, Ethan. She's all yours. But we get to watch." Mark Tennyson hauled Immanuel Stoner around and knocked him to the ground next to his wife. "Maybe he can give you some hints as to what pleasures her most. Bet she's never had a man half as good as me."

"Who cares about her? It's been well nigh a month since I had me a woman. I'm beginnin' to feel the pressures buildin' up inside me till I'm ready to explode." Ethan Crain began unbuckling the gunbelt around his thick waist, intent clear even to Immanuel Stoner.

"You swine! You can't—"

Jeb knocked the angry man to the ground, then kicked him hard enough to roll him over. Immanuel Stoner lay stunned, his eyes refusing to focus. He made strange gurgling noises, as if something deep inside had busted.

"He ain't no fun no more. Get the boy. Let him watch as you do his ma." Marcus Tennyson went to fetch David Stoner, pulling him from the back of the wagon. The youth's eyes were wide and his face pale in fright.

"You won't get away with this," David said. Nobody paid any heed to his ineffectual struggles. He licked his lips as the Tennysons pushed him to the ground beside his father.

"We *are* gettin' away with it," bragged Ethan Crain. "We done got away with more 'n this for years. There's no lawman in these parts able to put us behind bars."

"You'll hang for this. I swear you will!" David Stoner's bravado faded when Ethan Crain lowered his pants and moved toward the fallen woman.

Slocum waited for Crain to drop his drawers to his ankles. That would limit his mobility enough to make him the target for the last shot he fired. First Jeb, Slocum decided, then the outlaw's brother. And then the raping cousin.

"Hold on, Ethan. Don't go startin' anything without her husband watchin'. It wouldn't be right." Jeb rolled Stoner over and slapped him back to consciousness. "There you are. See how a real man pleasures your woman."

"No, you can't. Don't. You're animals."

"Seems to be what the little lady needs," Crain said. "She's been puttin' up with a eunuch all these years." He rolled the word "eunuch" off his tongue as if it were dipped in honey.

Slocum saw that he couldn't get a good shot at either of the Tennysons since they'd shifted positions. Ethan Crain blocked them from direct fire. Slocum knew he had a few more minutes. Lottie Stoner wasn't in much danger, not yet. The outlaws wanted to lord it over their captives and make them squirm. Men like the Tennysons enjoyed torture more than they did anything else.

Getting into the tumbledown general store gave Slocum just the right angle. He settled down and got Jeb Tennyson in his sights. He started to squeeze back on the rifle's trigger and eliminate one of the yahoos when David Stoner let out a shriek of pure outrage and drove his shoulder into Jeb Tennyson's middle.

GHOST TOWN 69

The outlaw doubled over and went tumbling ass over teakettle. Stoner didn't stop his attack. Swinging wildly, he drove Marcus Tennyson away and then grabbed for Ethan Crain.

Slocum had lost his chance at the Tennysons. He hoped he wasn't too late to get Crain.

"You can't do that. You can't rape my mother!" David Stoner shrieked.

"Why not?" Ethan Crain asked in a deceptively mild voice. "You're not man enough to stop me." From a vest pocket, Crain whipped out a small pistol, maybe a double-barreled derringer, and fired pointblank into David Stoner's face.

The boy jerked upright and then toppled backward to the ground like a felled tree.

8

"Hey, don't go killin' anyone yet!" protested Jeb Tennyson. He grabbed his cousin's arm and jerked the derringer upward. The second shot echoed through Buzzard Flats. Slocum still held his fire, waiting to see if he couldn't get a better shot. He worried now that Ethan Crain might take it into his head to keep killing. Once a man like that tasted blood, one death was never enough.

"Yeah, Ethan. Lookee here what I got." Mark Tennyson held Sarah Stoner so her arm was bent behind her in an arm lock. She struggled fiercely but couldn't get free. Any thought Slocum had of shooting the outlaws from hiding now faded. He could never kill one or even two of the men without the third injuring Sarah.

All three men waved their guns around, pointing them at Sarah and Immanuel Stoner and finally at the sobbing Lottie Stoner. Slocum sank back, cursing the turn of fate. He didn't dare shoot or the Tennysons would kill another of the Stoner family. Slocum's—and Sarah's—best chance was for him to bide his time, no matter how hard that might be, and wait for the right opportunity. He felt passing bad about David Stoner's death, but the boy had been foolish.

GHOST TOWN 71

Running square on at Ethan Crain was a damned stupid thing to do. Still, Slocum felt a little responsible. He could have killed Crain and let Immanuel and Lottie Stoner take their chances. Slocum heaved a sigh of disgust. He knew that was completely wrong. If Sarah was in danger, he'd never do anything to bring her to grief.

Even if he let the Tennysons kill her mother and father and throw them in a common grave with her brother, he'd never let them hurt her. But he had to make the attempt to save them. Benjamin Carter had hired him to scout, and he had promised his old friend that he'd fetch the Stoners and get them back to the wagon train.

Slocum had never thought he'd be in a position to pick and choose which of them he wanted to bring back alive.

"I want her," Ethan Crain said again, moving toward Lottie Stoner. Slocum considered letting the outlaw start in with the woman. His two cousins might get so unruly watching the rape that Slocum would have his chance to cut them down where they stood. It would take Crain a few seconds to get his wits back. That might be all Slocum would need to put a bullet in that owlhoot's belly.

Slocum decided that watching all three die a slow, lingering death was something he might enjoy. He just needed the chance to make it come true.

"Let her be, Ethan," said Marcus Tennyson. "We can keep them for a long, long time. Sorta relish the notion of what it would be like." The expression on Tennyson's face turned Slocum's belly.

"Why wait?" Ethan Crain stared from Lottie to her daughter. Slocum's finger twitched on the trigger of his Winchester. A move toward Sarah would bring instant death, no matter what it meant for her parents.

He got his chance when Ethan Crain turned slightly. Slocum could put one bullet through the yahoo's head, then get Jeb Tennyson before his cousin hit the ground. That would leave Sarah safe for a moment, maybe long enough for Slocum to cut down Marcus Tennyson.

His finger came back smoothly and the hammer fell—with a dull click.

For a moment Slocum wasn't sure what had happened. He expected the kick of the Winchester and the report, but all he heard was the click.

Cursing, he levered the round from the chamber, only to have it hang in the chamber. The rim had bent, causing the round to misfire. Now he had it jammed in the receiver. Dropping the rifle, his hand went for his Colt Navy, ready to finish the job with his six-shooter.

But Crain backed off. Rather than try a risky shot at this distance with a hand gun, Slocum sank back behind the pile of timbers he used as a hiding spot.

"Why hurry? We got all the time in the world. Hell, it's been a couple years since we were in Buzzard Flats. Seems we done up and kilt the whole damned town. I want to walk around and enjoy the sight of this goddamned place being deserted." Mark Tennyson puffed up his chest and strutted about like the cock of the walk.

"Mark's right," spoke up his brother. "We can savor winning over the lot of them, then have these ladies as our dessert. Our just desserts, I'd say." Jeb laughed uproariously at his joke, and his brother and cousin joined in.

Slocum didn't think much of their humor, but Marcus and Ethan went along with the notion of tying the Stoners to different wagon wheels. Slocum was glad to see that Lottie and Immanuel were on this side and Sarah was put on the other side, away from where the three outlaws punched each other on the shoulder and boasted loudly of their conquests.

Slipping from the shell of a store, he circled and came up on the far side of the wagon. Sarah sat on the ground, her hands secured to the wagon wheel and her head bowed. Slocum thought she sobbed silently, though he couldn't be sure. The crescent moon ducked behind increasingly heavy storm clouds and bathed her in shadow.

From somewhere Jeb got a bottle of whiskey, and the trio started in to heavy drinking. Slocum weighed his chances. If the three passed out, it would be easy to slip into their camp and cut their throats one at a time. He touched the heavy hunting knife sheathed at the small of his back. The thick-bladed weapon hadn't seen such useful duty in a coon's age.

Almost as the idea of finishing them individually came to mind, Slocum heard Jeb complain, "Don't go spillin' that, Ethan. It's the only bottle we got."

"I'll do any damn thing I want. There!"

Slocum winced as the tinkle of breaking glass reached his ears. Any hope he might have had of them drinking themselves into oblivion just vanished. They might be liquored up, but that made them more dangerous, not unconscious.

Wasting time now meant the slim chance he had of rescuing Sarah would pass. He moved forward, a silent shadow moving in deeper shadow. Her head snapped up and her mouth opened. Slocum clamped a hand over it and whispered, "Hush. Don't go letting them know I'm here."

"John, they killed David!"

"We don't want them doing that to you." Slocum didn't bother telling her he had seen the murder. She might get to asking questions about why he didn't stop the outlaws, and Slocum wasn't inclined to argue his tactics. He might have played the situation differently, but that was past now and no amount of jawing would change it.

"My ma and pa," protested Sarah. "They have them tied on the other side of the wagon. Get them free, too."

"First you. Then we'll see what has to be done." Slocum drew his sharp knife across the thick ropes holding Sarah's wrists. The hemp parted with a sigh. She threw trembling arms around his neck and hugged him close. Slocum liked the feel of a woman this close, but he kept thinking of what might happen if the Tennysons came around the wagon and saw him.

"We get away and then worry over your folks," Slocum said, disengaging the woman and pulling her away from the wagon. "Be as quiet as a church mouse. I don't want to shoot it out with three of them." He regretted leaving his rifle behind in the store, but it would take a bit of work to clear the round from the chamber and get the Winchester into working condition again.

Until then, Slocum had to depend on his Colt.

He and Sarah got to the rear of a deserted but intact store, an undertaker's parlor from the look of it, and sank down inside behind a table holding a pair of pine coffins. Sarah was panting harshly, as if she had run miles and miles. Slocum's own heart was running fast, but it came from anticipation rather than fear. He wanted those three—bad.

"I know them," he told Sarah. "I crossed them a few years ago. They rustled a herd I was ramroding. The owner wasn't any too pleased when I lost every last head. He blamed me, though it wasn't my fault." Slocum still carried more than a touch of bitterness over that accusation. He and two others had been rounding up strays when the Tennyson gang made their raid on the herd. They had run off half and stampeded the other half over a cliff and into a ravine. What they hadn't stolen they had killed.

"They'll kill my parents, John. I saw how they murdered David. They . . . just shot him." She shivered, as if she'd never seen a man die before. And Slocum had to allow that Sarah might not have. No matter, that had been her brother and she was permitted to mourn a while for him. Slocum hoped it didn't go on too long. He thought he'd need her support if Immanuel and Lottie Stoner were to be rescued.

"We can stop them, but we have to be cagy. Just walking on up to them and asking for mercy isn't going to work. They're stone killers, the lot of 'em."

"What do we do?"

"They don't know I'm here. They tried to bushwhack me in the woods. Maybe they think they succeeded." Slocum frowned as he spoke. The Tennysons had to know he wasn't dead. The mysterious stranger who had saved his hide by driving them off would be a thorn in their sides, too. Still, the outlaws didn't act as if they had a care in the world. They had obviously blown through Buzzard Flats sometime in the past and counted the town's death as a notch on their six-guns.

He shrugged off guessing what these half-drunk desperados thought. They didn't seem any too balanced to Slocum. Pulling on Sarah, he worked his way around, down one alley and up

GHOST TOWN 75

another until he came to a spot near the saloon. For a moment, he thought the Tennysons had entered and were searching for more liquor.

"What's wrong, John?" Sarah clung to his arm. He moved her hand off his arm, to keep ready for anything that happened.

"I thought I heard voices in the saloon."

"I didn't hear anything. Where are we going?"

"Around to the general store, right across from where your folks are tied. My rifle jammed. I want to get it back and look through the debris and maybe find something for you to use."

"I don't know how to use a gun," Sarah said.

"Could you shoot someone if they were threatening your ma and pa? Could you shoot the one who gunned down your brother?" Slocum saw the grim resolve on the woman's face and knew the answer. She followed closely as he edged along behind the saloon and came to the general store where he had tried to ambush the Tennysons.

Picking his way through the fallen beams, he found his rifle. Getting the shell cleared was beyond him in the dark. Slocum started poking about in the debris, finding small items left behind. Working to the rear of the store, he found a large crate, its lid poorly nailed down. The smell of gun grease made his nose wrinkle. Slocum pulled at the lid.

The nails made a screeching noise he thought even the outlaws would hear. They were singing a bawdy ballad and didn't hear the racket. Slocum fumbled around inside the box and almost let out a whoop of glee.

"What is it, John? What did you find?"

"Another rifle. And ammunition." He pulled his treasure out and saw that rust had worked its way into the barrel. Firing the weapon might cause it to explode, but Slocum knew they'd have to take their chances. He didn't have time to examine or clean the rifle properly. He fitted the shells into the magazine and levered one into the firing chamber.

Sarah almost grabbed it from his hands. He stopped her.

"Be careful. Don't use this unless you have to. I don't know what condition it's in."

"I don't care. I want to . . . I want to kill them all!"

"We will," he promised her, "but we'll make sure your mother and father don't get killed along the way." Slocum thought hard. The general store didn't give as good a vantage as he'd hoped.

"Next door," he said finally. "We can get onto the saloon's second floor and shoot down on them. They'll have a harder time getting to cover. We might drive them off, even if we don't kill them."

"And save Ma and Father," Sarah finished, her eyes glowing. Slocum had seen this look before. Blood lust. He wanted to send her off, away from town and the temptation to have a death on her pretty head.

"I do the shooting," Slocum told her. "I know what I'm doing. If you go throwing lead around, you'll only spook 'em and put your parents in worse danger."

"All right," Sarah said softly, but the edge in her voice told of her change of heart. She had gone from being afraid of hurting anyone to seeing her brother murdered in cold blood. Now Sarah wanted to kill.

Slocum led the way from the general store, moving to the saloon. He paused, thinking they might have been dealt a better hand than they deserved. From inside the saloon came boisterous voices and the clink of shot glasses on the bar. The Tennysons had found liquor and would be easy prey.

Slipping to the rear door, Slocum looked around the doorframe into the saloon and blinked in surprise.

Although gaslights sputtered along the walls of the saloon, the room was empty. Empty and as silent as the grave.

"What's wrong, John? How did those lights get lit?" Sarah pushed past and into the saloon. Slocum followed, his six-shooter ready for action. There wasn't any danger because the Tennysons were still outside in the street. Slocum went to the front doors and peered out at the trio.

They were shooting their pistols wildly and laughing at their conquest. He saw them burst into the town jail and make a

GHOST TOWN 77

mock escape, then stagger along toward the bank.

"What are they doing?" asked Sarah.

"Looks to me as if they're playacting at robbing the town bank." Slocum judged his chances of getting back and rescuing the Stoners, then pushed the thought from his mind. The Tennysons never let their captives out of their sight for long. If a brother and a cousin went into the bank, one held back in the street.

"If they keep this up, we've got them," Slocum said. He figured to kill the one left in the street, then pin down the other two while Sarah rescued her parents. With a bit of planning, he might be able to plug all three of the owlhoots from the upstairs windows.

"I've never been in a saloon before," Sarah said in a voice laced with awe. "So this is what they look like." She spun around, as if dancing to music only she could hear. "And the stairs?"

"They lead to the cribs," Slocum said harshly. He worried that the Tennysons had turned on the gaslights and then gone off on their revelry. They might return. If they did, Sarah had to have her wits about her.

"The soiled doves worked up there, didn't they? You've been in such places of ill repute before, haven't you, John?" Sarah's face glowed as she stared up the rickety staircase.

"Spent some time in dance halls," Slocum allowed. "Does that bother you?" He found himself talking to thin air. Sarah had already gone up the stairs and was poking around in the rooms she found.

Slocum glanced outside and saw the situation with the outlaws hadn't changed much. They took turns pretending to rob stores and then arresting each other, only to break out of the jailhouse. Slocum edged back and then followed Sarah up the steps to the second floor. He wanted to get the Stoners free and clear out of Buzzard Flats. The longer he stayed here, the edgier he got.

"Are the rooms like you expected?" Slocum asked, seeing Sarah rummaging through wardrobes and dresser drawers. What she sought was beyond him. All he wanted was to plug a trio of bandits and be on his way back to Carter's wagon train.

"The rooms are so small," Sarah answered, "but all the Cyprians had to do was come up here for a few minutes with their . . . clients."

Slocum shook his head. Sarah edged around calling the women who lived in these coffin-sized rooms by their real professional title: whores. She seemed to get some forbidden thrill out of even being in the same room where the women had plied their trade.

"Look at this, John. Isn't it amazing?" Sarah held up a battered red satin gown trimmed in black lace. She held it up in front of her and it only came to mid-knee. Such daring amazed her. And the décolletage was scandalous for any proper lady. Sarah found it exciting.

"We've got work to do," Slocum told her. "I'm going to see where those yahoos have gotten off to, and then I'm going to need you and that rifle pretty quick." He pointed to the rusty rifle Sarah had dropped on the dusty bed.

Slocum went to the side window and peered out, getting a good view of the wagon where the Stoners were tied. But he couldn't see any of the Tennyson gang. He heard their sporadic gunfire and loud whoops. They might even have found more liquor from the guzzling noises being made, but Slocum couldn't be sure. He settled down, rifle on the window ledge. He used his knife to pry out the bullet jammed in the action, tossed the bent cartridge away, then levered in a new round. He made sure the Winchester worked easily before reloading it. There might be only one or two good shots when the outlaws showed their worthless faces again.

The third shot would be the one deciding the Stoners' fate. He didn't dare let any of the killers survive his first attack or the sodbusters' lives were forfeit.

A scraping sound behind him made Slocum whirl around, his Colt Navy swinging up. He stopped and his eyes widened when he saw Sarah standing in the doorway. She had changed into the red and black outfit.

"Do you like it? It feels so naughty." Sarah pirouetted, making the flouncy skirt spin outward. Her breasts were barely held into the tight bodice, but the woman's legs caught Slocum's full attention. The faster she turned, the more the skirt lifted. She wasn't wearing anything under it.

"Is this the way the soiled doves go to work? So they can be ready for their next gentleman?" Sarah lifted the front of the skirt more and more, aware that she held Slocum's full attention. Only when the barest flash of furry, dark brown triangle between her white thighs appeared did she stop lifting.

"We can't—" Slocum swallowed hard. It was hard to concentrate on making the best shot possible with Sarah dressed like this—and acting as she did.

"Would I make a good dance-hall girl? Would you pay money for someone like me?" She moved closer, the satin dress whispering as she moved. Sarah sat on the dusty mattress behind Slocum, blocking the path from the room. As if he'd want to go anywhere.

"You're about the prettiest woman I ever saw. And you're too good to ever work in a cathouse. You're—" She silenced him by throwing her arms around his neck and pulling him close. Her lips crushed into his. Slocum returned the kiss instinctively, then tried to push away.

"We got trouble down there. Your folks. The Tennysons."

"Nothing's going to change for a while," Sarah said huskily. "Would you pay money for me, John? Am I *that* pretty?"

"Pretty's got nothing to do with a man paying for a woman," he said.

"I want you, John. Now!" Sarah lay back on the bed. Her short skirt flowed into the air, again giving him a view of paradise. Her breasts heaved up and down as she breathed heavily.

Slocum reached over and touched one of the laces on her bodice. He tugged gently on the cord and her top fell open, spilling out twin mounds of succulent snowy-white flesh. Slocum tried to resist but found his resolve weakening. What did it matter if he killed the Tennysons now or later? They'd never find him and Sarah upstairs in the cribs.

He bent over and lightly kissed one cherry-red nipple. Sarah moaned softly and cupped her own breast, holding it up for his attention. He kissed it again, this time licking a mite and nipping with his teeth. Sarah groaned louder and pulled him down. He took most of the breast into his mouth, licking and biting and sucking until Sarah was thrashing about in delight.

"I want more, John. I want you to take me like a whore. Do me like a whore!"

She ran her hands down the front of his shirt, tearing at the buttons, fumbling to get his fly open. Slocum dropped his gunbelt and laid his Winchester next to it on the floor. Sarah was busy undressing him all the while. By the time she got his fly open, his manhood popped out, long and tall and proud.

"I want it. *I want it.*" Sarah leaned over and licked lightly, starting at the base and racing to the tip. A thrill went through Slocum unlike anything he'd ever felt. Just the sight of Sarah Stoner drove him crazy with lust. And what she did poured kerosene onto the fires building within him.

"Can't stand it a second longer," he told her, rolling onto the bed and trying to fit himself between her legs. To his surprise, Sarah twisted away.

"Not that way. I want you to take me like you would a harlot." She moved so that she was on hands and knees, her smooth, rounded butt wiggling enticingly in the air. She looked back at Slocum and urged him to climb onto the bed behind her.

The bed was too rickety for it to support his full weight. Slocum stood beside the bed, and put his hands on Sarah's hips. Then pulled the beautiful brunette around so his hard length slid between her warm thighs. She shook all over, like a leaf in a high wind.

Then she rammed her ass back into the curve of his groin, trying to bury him full length in her heated interior. Slocum was out of position and his cock danced down the woman's greased slit. The feeling was pleasurable for both of them, but he needed more.

And so did Sarah.

He pulled back slightly, lined up and then leaned forward. He drove into her heated core so fast that the room spun around him. He hung onto her bucking hips for support. Widening his stance helped. Pulling back a few inches, Slocum savored the feeling all around his turgid tip.

He shoved back in balls-deep. Sarah went berserk, tossing her head like a filly cavorting in a meadow, moaning and sobbing and uttering obscene things that he never expected to hear from her lips. But everything she did made him even hotter. He had to possess her totally.

Moving faster and faster, he felt carnal friction burning his length. Sarah gasped and writhed and then convulsed as intense passion seized control of her. Slocum gasped. It felt as if he had been caught in a mine, the roof crashing down on him. But no mine was ever so clinging and warm and demanding.

He fell into the ages-old rhythm of a man loving a woman and lost all control. The hot tide exploded from his balls and burst forth, triggering another intense shivering in Sarah's body. Her arms gave out and she fell facedown onto the bed, her breasts rubbing along the coarse blanket on the mattress. As Slocum continued to stroke, Sarah ground her upper body down harder and harder until a third wave of complete fervor blasted through her.

Only then did she pull away from Slocum, slipping onto the bed, a contented smile on her face.

"That's the way they always make love, isn't it, John?"

"No," he said, shaken from the intensity of the ardor he had just experienced. Slocum couldn't rightly remember how many women he had been with, but it had never been this potent. "This was better."

He reached out and laid his hand on her flushed cheek. Sarah rolled onto her side, her breasts flopping out. Slocum tweaked first one blood-engorged nipple and then the other, realizing how his need for this incredible woman was building again.

Boisterous laughter from downstairs made him pull up his pants even as he reached for his six-shooter. The

Tennysons weren't going to catch him with his pants down.

Still hitching up his drawers, Slocum went to kill himself some outlaws.

9

Slocum paused to get his gunbelt cinched up around his waist, then continued down the hall. He waited at the top of the stairs, not wanting to blunder down into the Tennysons' guns. He heard their raucous laughter and the clink of glasses. Someone swore when liquor was spilled. Slocum knew he had them. They would be too intent on boozing it up to notice him getting a bead on them.

Cocking his Colt, Slocum started down the stairs. He tested each step for creaking. Warning them was the last thing he wanted to do. The sound of gunfire wouldn't alert whoever had been left guarding the Stoners. The ruckus they kicked up was so noisy a war could be fought and the third member of the gang would never know.

His feet would be seen if he kept moving too much more down the stairs. Slocum took a breath, then dropped suddenly, his six-shooter swinging around the corner of the wall. His finger was coming back on the trigger when he froze.

The room, lit by the guttering gaslamps in sconces on the walls, was empty.

"Can't be," Slocum said to himself. He dropped a few more steps, sure that he had missed the Tennysons somehow. He had heard their raucous laughter and the sounds of drinking. The Colt swung back and forth, ready to drill any outlaw in its sights. How the desperadoes had left so fast, Slocum couldn't say.

Cautiously descending, he looked over the bar. He half expected to be staring down the muzzle of Ethan Crain's derringer or one of his cousin's six-shooters. Only cobwebs and undisturbed dust stretched behind the long bar. Swinging about, Slocum worried that they had ducked out the back way.

But why play with him like this? They seemed oblivious to any threat he might pose. The outlaws were intent on frightening their captives and shooting up Buzzard Flats.

"John, what's wrong?" came Sarah's worried question. "You rushed out so fast, I thought maybe I'd done something wrong."

"Didn't you hear them? They were in here, drinking, laughing. But they vanished like ghosts." Slocum swallowed hard, then got mad at himself for even thinking the Tennyson gang wasn't real. The bullets they had thrown at him were real. David Stoner's death was as ugly as it was real. And weren't Lottie and Immanuel Stoner still tied to their wagon's wheel?

If Slocum hadn't rescued Sarah, she would still be a prisoner. There wasn't anything supernatural about Ethan Crain and his two cousins.

But Sarah's words chilled him, nonetheless.

"I didn't hear anything from down here, John. They're still outside, shooting up the town. There wasn't a sound from down here."

"I'm getting too high-strung for my own good," Slocum said ruefully. He holstered his Colt Navy, then finished buttoning his pants and getting his clothes settled just right. He pulled his six-shooter again and went to the saloon door, peering out. The Tennysons were at the other end of town, blasting holes in still-standing walls.

Slocum shook his head. No matter what Sarah said, he *had* heard voices in this room. If it wasn't the Tennyson gang, who had it been? His gaze worked across the floor, trying to piece together the clues telling him what men had walked across the dusty floor. He had been here several times. The Tennysons had entered, looking for booze. And Sarah. She had wandered about.

The dust was too stirred up for him to get any idea how many people had come and gone in the past few hours. The few cobwebs that had been disturbed were all near doorways. Slocum went to one of the gaslights and stared at the brass fittings.

"Who turned the lights up?" he wondered aloud. "And why is the gas still working after almost two years?"

Slocum hit the floor when several rounds came winging through the open door and embedded in the wall by his head. He spun agilely and wormed around behind an overturned table, waiting for the rush of outlaws coming into the saloon to finish the job they had started.

"Are you all right, John?" Sarah started down the stairs. Slocum found it hard to concentrate on the outlaws when she was dressed as she was. He saw up her skirt, and she hadn't bothered relacing her tight bodice.

"Get back up there," he said harshly. "They must have spotted me."

"I don't think so," she said, not obeying his order. Sarah came down and lightly crossed the floor, pressing against the wall and looking out a shattered window. "I can see them. One's still got a gun pressed to my father's head. The other two are inside the jailhouse. I can't tell what they are doing."

Slocum joined her and looked around the edge of the window. Whatever lead had come his way was accidental—incidental. Jeb and Mark Tennyson were enjoying themselves, not much caring where they shot.

"They haven't noticed you've escaped," Slocum said, thinking there might be a better way of getting Sarah's parents free. "If you divert Crain, I can plug him and we can both wait for the brothers to come out of the jailhouse."

"I don't know if I could, John. Things are happening so fast, and I've never shot anyone. I want to, I do! After they killed

David, I want to kill them. But I don't know if I can!" Sarah's voice rose to a wail. Slocum knew she was on the brink of crying. Pulling her to him, he held her until the burgeoning hysteria faded a mite.

He couldn't depend on her if the outlaws started shooting, and Slocum knew he would lose her if Ethan Crain or one of his cousins killed either her mother or father. Sarah would lose control and do something stupid that might get her gunned down.

"You go get back into your own clothes," Slocum said softly. "We'll get out the back and then you can take my horse and ride on out of Buzzard Flats. Go outside town a few miles and wait for me."

"But, John, I can't do that!" She looked up at him with those tear-filled, wide brown eyes. Slocum forced himself to keep staring into her eyes. The way her naked breasts tumbled out—and the dress with nothing under it!—diverted his attention from life-and-death matters.

"I'll be fine. If I'm not worrying about your safety, I can do a better job getting your ma and pa free." What Slocum wanted more than anything else was to get rid of the distraction Sarah provided him. He felt himself responding, wanting to take her in his arms, to take her again as he had upstairs.

"It's not right, but how can I argue? You know about these things. I'm just a silly ole farm girl."

"You're anything but a silly farm girl," he told her earnestly. "Now get changed, and bring back both rifles. I'll make sure they don't come blundering in here until you're ready."

For all the boldness Sarah had shown upstairs, she was now a frightened little girl. She hesitantly went up the stairs and into the crib where she had left her clothing. Slocum heard the murmurs of cloth moving as Sarah dropped the satin dance-hall-girl getup, interspersed with tiny sobs as if she had realized how she'd been acting. Slocum had never seen anything like that before.

And he wanted more.

Slocum hitched up his gunbelt and turned his attention back to the street. The Tennysons had finally discovered Sarah had escaped. Jeb walked to the middle of the street and called, "This is gonna be fun, girlie. We're comin' for you. When we find you, you're gonna pleasure all three of us all night long!"

Slocum judged the distance as being too far. He didn't want to give away his presence.

"Where are you, dearie? Come on out. Come to Jeb and get a nice surprise!" The drunken outlaw guffawed loudly and grabbed at his crotch.

Slocum whirled when he heard a sound behind him. Sarah stood at the foot of the stairs, a stricken expression on her face.

"I heard, John. They know you freed me. What will they do to Father and Ma?"

"They don't know I helped you get away. They think you did it on your own. We might be able to use that." Slocum's mind raced. The only conclusion he could come to, though, was getting Sarah out of Buzzard Flats. With her safely hidden outside town, he could come back and settle the score with the Tennysons.

"Come on out and get what you been hankerin' for all your life. You don't know what you're missin', girlie." Jeb Tennyson walked down the middle of the street, but as inviting a target as he was, Slocum didn't shoot. Ethan Crain held a six-shooter to Lottie Stoner's head. Any hint that his cousin was in trouble would loose Crain's sick need to wantonly kill.

"Out the back way," Slocum said. "We can get to my horse and be out of town while they're wasting time hunting for you. If they get too riled up, all three of them might come looking."

"You could save my folks then, couldn't you? All right. Let's go, but I feel like a sniveling coward for doing this."

Slocum said nothing. It was her father who was the coward. He would rather leave his home in Missouri than to let his daughter take up with a man he didn't approve of. Running never solved anything. Slocum had always faced up to his problems, even when it meant a world of woe for him.

The dead carpetbagger judge and his hired gun was only one link in a long chain of doing what was right. The law might not see it that way, but it felt right to John Slocum, and that was what counted. If he couldn't live with himself because of something he did, that was where the line had to be drawn.

It felt right, damned right, thinking on killing the Tennyson gang.

"Don't fret about it, Sarah," he told her. "There aren't men like you've come across before. Even if you pa thought Frank was something of a rowdy, the Tennysons put anything he might do to shame—unless you were talking about Frank James."

"No," Sarah said, smiling weakly. "I wasn't being courted by the likes of Frank James." Sarah stared at him and then impetuously kissed him. She had turned shy after her wanton moments upstairs in the cribs. Slocum didn't try to explain it. Buzzard Flats made people do crazy things.

He'd be glad to put the town at his back and never once look in its direction again.

"Nobody outside," Slocum said, casting a quick glance out the back door. He heard Jeb Tennyson caterwauling out in front of the saloon. They had left just in time. Slocum wondered how long this search for Sarah would go on before Ethan Crain or one of his cousins decided to flush the girl by threatening to shoot both her parents. When it happened, Slocum wanted to be far away.

"You can get them? You weren't able to before."

"I was worrying about your safety." Slocum dashed across the mouth of an alley, seconds before Marcus Tennyson stopped in the main street and looked down. Again Slocum's trigger finger got mighty itchy. A single easy shot would kill the outlaw.

And the Stoners, Slocum kept reminding himself. If Ethan Crain took it into his head to open fire, both of Sarah's parents were buzzard bait. Before that happened, Slocum figured Crain would try torturing his prisoners, hoping their pitiful cries would bring the escaped girl out of hiding.

Slocum froze when he sensed movement ahead. He lifted his Colt and waited for someone to show himself. If it was Jeb Tennyson, the man was a goner. Ethan Crain or no, Slocum was going to cut the man down. Jeb was as close to being the leader of the gang. Without him, the other two might argue a few seconds, giving Slocum the time he needed to finish the cleanup chores.

"What is it, John?" whispered Sarah, pressing close behind him. "Did you see something?"

"I don't know." Slocum lowered the six-shooter, wondering if his senses were failing. He had seen movement in the shadows, a tall man with a wide-brimmed, tall-crowned hat pinched in all around, Northern style. Slocum wore his Stetson with only the sides pinched in, like most other cowboys in the Southwest.

Other than the quick glimpse of the man's hat, Slocum hadn't gotten a good look at him. Moving forward, he poked around until he assured himself no one was there. Slocum had to keep telling himself Sarah wasn't seeing or hearing half of what he was—and she was the one frightened to death of what might happen.

"There's my horse," he said. "You go on and ride out. I'll lay an ambush for those sidewinders."

"John," Sarah said, stopping beside the Appaloosa. She bit her lower lip and struggled to say what was on her mind.

"Go on. It'll be all right. I'll get your ma and pa away unharmed."

"John, if you can't, I don't want you getting hurt. Save yourself, if it comes to that." Sarah gave him another quick kiss, more a peck this time, then struggled to get into the saddle. Slocum helped her up. She sat uncomfortably. Or was it only the tenseness hanging in the air between them that Slocum sensed?

"Go on. Let me get to my work." He hefted his Winchester and gave the rusty rifle to Sarah. "You might need this. Don't fire it unless you have to."

"I—" Sarah laid the rifle across her lap, turned her face, and kicked her heels a couple of times into the Appaloosa's flanks. The horse was slow to obey the gentle commands given by the woman, but the horse eventually started walking away from Buzzard Flats and into the night. Slocum watched for a moment, then turned to find a spot where he could cut down Ethan Crain.

He had decided a full frontal assault was the only possible way of saving the Stoners. The outlaws were too likely to start shooting if he tried anything less. He'd kill Ethan Crain, then gun down whichever of the Tennysons that came to see what the fuss was all about. Then he'd have them, too.

Working his way through the deserted town, Slocum found an old bookstore catty-corner from the wagon that afforded a good shot at Ethan Crain. The man twisted around nervously, shifting from foot to foot, even switching hands holding his six-gun. Slocum sighted in on Crain's heart, waiting for him to move the six-shooter from his right hand to his left. That would give a second or more to get off a second shot, should it be needed, when Crain couldn't kill either of his prisoners.

Just as Slocum was ready to fire, he heard movement that brought him up short.

"Let them go, you evil man!" Sarah came out of an alley, the rusted rifle in her shaking hands. "Don't make me kill you!"

"Well, well, what do we have here?" Ethan Crain stepped to one side, out of Slocum's line of fire and lifted his six-shooter.

Slocum cursed Sarah and he cursed the outlaws and he cursed himself for being in the wrong spot. He kicked through the debris around him, burst out the front door and started firing. To hell with accuracy. He had to distract Crain long enough to let Sarah get to safety.

"Run, Sarah!" Slocum yelled. "Get the hell out of here!" He fired five quick rounds until the Winchester came up empty. He dropped the rifle and drew his Colt, ready for a protracted fight.

"Yeah, Ethan, don't make the little lady kill you," came Mark Tennyson's mocking words from behind Slocum. "And don't make me kill you, cowboy. Put down that hogleg of yours."

GHOST TOWN 91

Slocum saw that Sarah had ducked back into a tumbledown building, safe for the moment. But Tennyson held his six-gun pointed squarely at Slocum's head. The slightest movement on his part, and Slocum knew he would be lying dead alongside David Stoner.

Slocum dropped his ebony-handled Colt Navy, wondering how much longer he was going to be alive. From the leering expression on Mark Tennyson's face, not much longer.

10

Slocum knew he was going to die, but the only consolation he had was that Sarah was safe—or as safe as she was likely to get. He swore at her for being so foolish as to ride back into town, thinking she could take on Ethan Crain and his outlaw cousins when Slocum was leery of tangling with them. And Slocum could only wonder why she hadn't come seeking him out instead of running smack-dab into the teeth of the gunman's pistol.

What could she have hoped to prove?

"Goodbye, cowboy. Or maybe we ought to let you live for a while longer. I enjoy watching snakes squirm around, with their heads cut off. Do you reckon it's true they don't die 'til sundown? Let's find out, you damned sidewinder." Tennyson cocked his six-shooter, aimed, and got ready to plug Slocum in the head.

Tennyson hesitated when he heard the pounding of horse's hooves from the far end of town.

Slocum tried to make his break but Tennyson barked, "Freeze. Don't go movin' or I will cut you down where you stand. Who's that comin' into this forlorn town? A friend of yours?"

GHOST TOWN   93

"I don't know who it is," Slocum answered truthfully. Sarah was hiding in the other direction, and he doubted Tennyson would get upset over his brother riding in. "Maybe it's the law."

"What do you know about the law?" snapped Tennyson. Slocum saw the outlaw's finger tense on the trigger, turning white with pressure. He didn't know why the outlaw's six-shooter didn't fire. "We done kilt the whole damn lot of lawmen in this town. We *kilt* Buzzard Flats!" The hysteria in Mark Tennyson's voice gave Slocum the chance to make his break.

When the outlaw looked back down the street at the approaching rider, Slocum ducked, grabbed his Colt and rolled into the doorway, partially sheltering himself from gunfire. To his surprise, Tennyson paid him no attention. He stared at the rider in complete disbelief—and terror.

"It cain't be you. You're dead, Kincaid. I kilt you myself!" Tennyson started shooting at the rider as Slocum started firing at the gunman. He saw one bullet blow off Tennyson's Stetson, but the other three rounds missed by a country mile. Tennyson had shaken himself out of his fear and was running for cover.

"Giddyup!" came the loud cry from the direction of the Stoner's wagon. Slocum saw Ethan Crain in the box, whipping the oxen to motion. He had left the Stoners tied to the wagon wheels. As the wagon pulled out, they began flopping around, trying to keep from being pulled under the deadly wheels. Only the slowness of the oxen saved the Stoners from being crushed to death.

Slocum stood and got off a shot in Ethan Crain's direction, but Mark Tennyson opened up on him and drove him back. They both seemed to be firing in two directions at the same time, and doing a piss-poor job of it.

Slocum took the time to reload, watching as the rider simply rode on, as if Tennyson's bullets meant nothing to him. The horse shied a mite, but it was trained good enough not to spook. The rider—Tennyson had called him Kincaid—halted in front of the undertaker's and turned slowly, as if seeing Buzzard Flats for the first time.

The cylinder snapped back into Slocum's Colt Navy and the six-shooter came up, hunting for a good target. Slocum hesitated when his sights fixed on Kincaid. The man had dismounted and walked slowly down the middle of the street, oblivious to the bullets kicking up tiny dust devils around him. Slocum thought such luck was impossible until he got a better look at Mark Tennyson.

The man had turned a pasty white, and his hands shook so bad it was impossible for him to aim straight. If he'd been locked inside a barn, he couldn't have hit a wall.

"What's with that gent?" Slocum wondered aloud. Kincaid didn't seem anything special. He was tall, gaunt to the point of emaciation and was so pale he might have spent the last ten years inside Yuma Penitentiary far from the touch of the sun. Slocum had seen such pallor only on convicts and dead men. Kincaid wore a tall hat, battered and filled with holes. His shirt was plain cotton and his trousers were canvas duck and, like his hat, had seen better days. Clods of dirt clung to the legs and fell off as he moved.

Slocum almost laughed at the deliberate way Kincaid hitched up his gunbelt and turned toward Marcus Tennyson.

"I'm calling you out, Tennyson. Come meet your maker!"

"Go to hell, Kincaid! You ain't never gonna get me!" Tennyson fired recklessly, hitting nothing. Kincaid stood his ground.

"He's heading for the general store," Slocum shouted to Kincaid. "He's hightailin' it!"

Kincaid must have heard the shouted warning. He moved to his right, instinctively knowing where Tennyson ran. The gaunt man cast only a thin shadow, but Slocum felt a chill run down his spine as he watched the deliberate way Kincaid went after Tennyson. He wouldn't want Kincaid on his trail.

Slocum found himself torn between helping Kincaid run down Mark Tennyson and going after Ethan Crain. The man was driving the wagon out of town, taking the Stoners with it. They wouldn't last long if the outlaw kept driving. And then there was Sarah. Where had she gotten off to after Slocum had warned her away?

More gunfire decided Slocum, maybe not for the best. He ran into the street, intent on finding Kincaid and helping him run Mark Tennyson to ground. Slocum figured the tall man had to be the law. If they teamed up, they stood a better chance against the outlaws than either did separately. Colt clutched firmly in his steady grip, Slocum went hunting for Tennyson.

He swung about, going into a crouch when he heard a soft noise down one alley. His six-shooter centered on Kincaid's chest—and Kincaid's hogleg was trained on him.

"I'm Slocum. Tennyson tried to kill me. His cousin's taken a couple sodbusters prisoner."

"Ethan Crain." The name came out flat and dead. Slocum stared into Kincaid's eyes and saw only desolation there. It was as if something vital had long since died within the man. Only arctic cold remained of any more temperate emotion.

"He's the one. Jeb Tennyson is around town somewhere, too." Slocum didn't rise from the crouch. For all he knew, Kincaid was the Tennysons' partner, perhaps one they had double-crossed.

"What do you want, Slocum?" The flatness of the words took Slocum by surprise. For a man so determined to go after the outlaws that he ignored bullets flying around him, Kincaid surely was a cold fish.

"To help. We get Mark Tennyson, then we both go after Ethan Crain. If we rescue the sodbusters, we might talk about finding Jeb Tennyson and bringing him to justice."

This produced the first real expression on Kincaid's face. The corners of his mouth curled slightly, then he broke into a loud guffaw.

"That's rich. Justice. There's no way those owlhoots can be brought to justice. I just want to kill them."

"Seems mighty equitable to me, killing them. You the law?"

Kincaid reached over and touched his vest, where a star might have rode high. He shook his head slowly, and the grin faded from his lips. He started to speak but another flight of lead came winging its way down the alley, driving even the implacable thin man, to cover.

"I'm gonna kill you this time, Kincaid. I'm gonna do it. And you ain't never gonna see another sunset." Tennyson followed his boasts with quick, poorly-aimed rounds that made Slocum wonder if the fright was gone from the outlaw yet.

Slocum wiggled forward and came to rest beside Kincaid. The tall man hunkered down, trying to keep out of the line of fire. He looked at Slocum and said, "You bought yourself a passel of trouble. Why don't you get on out of here and let me have them?"

"That's a mighty appealing offer," Slocum allowed, "but I want a piece of him, too." After all the outlaws had done to the Stoner family, it was the least Slocum could do to pay back some of the misery. "And I reckon I owe you for pulling my fat out of the fire. Back in the forest outside of town."

"Suit yourself. This is going to get bloody." Kincaid leaned out and started firing. He stood and walked the six-gun blazing. To Slocum's surprise, this flushed Tennyson from his hidey-hole at the end of the alley. The outlaw ran as if all the demons of hell were nipping at his heels.

Slocum reloaded the rounds he had fired, then joined Kincaid in his search for Tennyson. He couldn't help looking around uneasily, wondering what had become of Jeb Tennyson. The brothers stuck together like flypaper. Having Jeb come up to backshoot him wasn't something Slocum wanted to contend with much longer.

"Where'd that sidewinder get off to?" Slocum asked, trying to find Mark Tennyson. Kincaid said nothing. He kept walking, reloading as he went. Slocum had never seen a man this fearless—or this stupid. Kincaid paid no attention to possible danger. He moved like some elemental force of nature, and this spooked Tennyson again.

Slocum fired at the fleeing outlaw, before Kincaid could finish reloading and get off a shot. Tennyson stumbled and clutched his left leg. Slocum had winged him, but not seriously enough to stop the desperado.

Kincaid snapped his cylinder back into his six-shooter and began firing again.

"We got him," Slocum called to Kincaid, when he saw Tennyson scrambling into the tumbledown livery behind an equally decrepit hotel. "The back door is nailed shut. He'll have to get out the front or pry loose a wall board to get out."

"He's mine. I'm laying claim on him." Kincaid fired until his six-shooter was empty and kept walking, reloading as he stopped in front of the stable where Mark Tennyson had taken refuge. Slocum approached slowly, keeping an eye skinned for Jeb Tennyson. The outlaw wasn't anywhere to be seen.

Slocum moved so he could watch the side and back of the stables, waiting for Tennyson to make an escape. What happened startled Slocum.

"I'm waiting for you, Marcus. Come on out and die like a man. It's more'n you ever allowed me and mine." Kincaid widened his stance and stood like a statue, his hand resting lightly on his holster. The wind blew past him gently, but Kincaid didn't notice. Not a muscle twitched; not an eye blinked. Kincaid simply waited, even if it meant standing exposed to Tennyson's fire for all eternity.

Mark Tennyson came from the stable, clutching his six-shooter so tight he shook. He'd sweat so hard his shirt was soggy, and a muscle spasmed under his left eye.

"You don't have to put your gun into its holster," Kincaid said in a cold voice. "Just raise it and fire, when you want."

Slocum might have seen a faster draw in his day, but he couldn't remember when. All Tennyson had to do was lift his six-shooter and fire. Kincaid drew, cocked his six-gun, aimed, and fired before Tennyson got his gun halfway up to its target.

Kincaid's slug hit square in the middle of Tennyson's face, turning it to a sunken pit. Slocum saw the outlaw stumble back and then fall, arms outstretched to land heavily. His six-shooter dropped beside his body, discharging and sending a bullet singing off into the distance.

Slocum turned toward Kincaid. The man stood as still as a statue again, his six-shooter smoking. As if dipped in molasses, Kincaid thrust his gun back into its holster. He didn't move for almost a minute, as if savoring Tennyson's death. But Slocum saw no triumph on Kincaid's face. He saw nothing but hollowness.

"He's mine," Kincaid said softly, then walked over to the fallen outlaw. Slocum thought he was past surprise. What Kincaid did then startled him more than if the man had scalped his enemy.

Kincaid pulled out a thin-bladed knife and pressed it against Tennyson's ring finger. A quick cut and the finger popped free. Slocum walked closer to watch what happened then. From the severed finger Kincaid took a thick gold wedding ring and slipped it onto his own hand.

The gold band was too large by half on Kincaid's skeletal finger, but the gunman didn't seem to notice. He tossed away Tennyson's finger and stood.

"I got work to do. The others are mine, too."

"They've got prisoners. They're holding the Stoner family hostage, leastwise Ethan Crain is. He had them tied to their wagon."

"So it was Crain who drove on out of Buzzard Flats?" Kincaid shook his head, as if considering how much longer his job would take. "I'll stop him."

"How are you going to keep him from killing the sodbusters?" Slocum heard more in Kincaid's words than had been uttered. Kincaid didn't give two hoots about anything but killing Ethan Crain and his remaining cousin. If the Stoners died along the way, it wouldn't much bother him.

"Dead men don't usually kick up much of a fuss," Kincaid told him.

"Wait!" Slocum hurried alongside the determined man. "If you go after him, Crain will kill his hostages. He's one mean son of a bitch."

"I'm meaner," Kincaid said. And Slocum didn't doubt it. Slocum almost ran to keep up with Kincaid's resolute pace. He glanced around, wanting to call out for Sarah. The lovely woman could change Kincaid's mind about how he went about killing Ethan Crain, but Slocum didn't see her. He worried that Jeb Tennyson might have caught her, then pushed the notion from his head.

If the outlaw had taken Sarah prisoner, he would be using her as a shield to come after the man who had just cut down his brother. Slocum had to deal with Kincaid right away or there might be sorry news for the young woman when she did poke her head out from her hiding place.

"Give me a few minutes. Let me try to get the sodbusters away safely. I don't much care who kills Ethan Crain, but I don't want to see the man and woman harmed."

Kincaid stopped abruptly and looked at Slocum. The tall, haggard man frowned slightly, as if thinking hard.

"What are they to you? Relatives?"

"I feel responsible for them. They got lost from a wagon train I'm scouting for."

Slocum didn't think this argument would carry any weight with Kincaid. To his amazement, it did. Kincaid nodded slowly.

"It's hard being responsible for others," the gaunt man allowed. "You got ten minutes to go after them. Then all hell's going to be out for lunch."

Staring into Kincaid's deep-sunk eyes, Slocum believed him. He hurried off to run down Ethan Crain and get the Stoners back before the real killing started.

11

Slocum slowed his headlong run when he drew even with the sheriff's office. Something made him go into the jailhouse to look around. The walls were filled with holes, recent ones put there by the Tennyson gang hurrahing the place, but he wasn't interested in the bullet-ridden wood. The roof had fallen in, but the sheriff's desk and everything on it was strangely intact, as if a servant had come in every morning to dust and straighten.

A stack of papers revealed nothing. Slocum rummaged through the desk drawers, having to force two open against their brass locks. Inside he found more paperwork. He glanced at the faces staring up at him from a dozen wanted posters but saw neither his face nor those of the Tennysons. The sheriff hadn't been interested in just any criminal. From the look of the age-yellowed posters, he had concentrated on those murdering and stealing horses.

Slocum found keys to the lockup in the rear of the jail, but they didn't interest him enough to take them and go poke through the cells. In his day he'd seen more than his share of cages. Dropping heavily into the chair behind the desk, Slocum sat for a moment, wondering what the last sheriff in Buzzard Flats had seen.

Reaching out, Slocum pulled a triangular block of wood across the desk. It seemed out of place under the stack of papers. Turning it around he saw the sheriff's name carved into the pine wood plaque. Somehow, the letters cut into the wood with loving care wasn't completely unexpected: Abe Kincaid.

"So you were sheriff of Buzzard Flats before it fell apart," Slocum mused. He pushed away from the desk and looked to the rack mounted on the wall beside the desk. All the rifles and shotguns had long since been removed, but he found a half-filled box of cartridges that might fit his Winchester. Slocum tucked the cartridges into his pockets, trying to remember what had become of his rifle. If he was going to tackle Ethan Crain head-on, he would need that trusty weapon.

Slocum didn't have to check the watch riding in his vest pocket to know the time allotted him by Sheriff Kincaid was running out. He couldn't sit around while that determined and utterly fearless gunman wanted the Tennyson gang brought down. Since Kincaid wasn't wearing a badge, Slocum figured he was now just a private citizen—but one anxious to stop the outlaws and their murdering ways.

Stopping in the jail's door, Slocum looked up and down Buzzard Flats' main street. Only silence greeted him. He saw nothing of Sarah Stoner, and he counted this as a good sign. After her crazy attempt to rescue her parents, the woman was better off hiding somewhere and leaving the fighting to him.

Slocum dashed across the street, wary of becoming a target for Jeb Tennyson. The outlaw would turn berserk when he found out Kincaid had killed his brother. Slocum had seldom seen a fairer fight, or one in which the victor had gone to such lengths to give the dead man an even chance. Mark Tennyson had had his six-shooter out. All he had to do was lift it and fire, and Kincaid had still bested him. That wouldn't count for much with Jeb, though.

Reaching the far side of the street, Slocum began going through the broken-down husks of the buildings, hunting for his Winchester. Finally finding it, he put a few of the shells taken from the sheriff's office into the magazine, then headed directly out of town to find Ethan Crain and the Stoners.

Slocum didn't have far to go. Crain had stopped the wagon just outside Buzzard Flats, but he had done more and this bothered Slocum. Immanuel and Lottie Stoner were no longer tied to the wagon wheels. Before he rushed in, guns blazing, Slocum would have to find what had happened to the sodbusters. He moved slowly, eyes taking in every detail of the wagon.

The Conestoga listed a mite, the result of a poorly-fashioned axle. The wagon might have made it back to Carter's wagon train where it could have been fixed properly, but Slocum wasn't too concerned about that. The occupants were in real trouble—or dead.

Slocum didn't turn when he heard soft movement behind him. He kept his rifle pointing toward the wagon but rested it on a pile of boards heaped in front of him. With a swift movement, he whirled about, Colt coming out of his holster. He might have been a shade slower than Abe Kincaid, but he was twice as fast as Sarah Stoner.

He caught the woman in his arms and shoved her to the ground. Sarah struggled and started to protest, then bit back her angry words when Slocum kept his six-shooter pointed at her face.

"Don't go making any sounds," he told her. Slocum rocked back, letting Sarah sit up.

"Why did you knock me down? That wasn't very gentlemanly of you, John." Sarah tried brushing herself off, but the dirt and mud caking her blouse and skirt made that impossible. She only smeared the filth around even worse.

"I told you to ride on out and wait for me. If you hadn't come back hooting and hollering like you did, I might have got Ethan Crain."

"He drove away with my parents tied to the wheels! He's a terrible man!"

Slocum snorted in disgust. It had taken a powerful lot of convincing for the woman to reach that conclusion. Crain had shot down her brother like a mad dog. She had to know the kind of men they faced in the Tennyson gang. He wondered if her strange behavior meant she had gone a mite crazy in the head. Slocum had seen it before, men doing things they never quite remembered later.

"We don't have much time. The town sheriff wants Crain and Jeb Tennyson, and he doesn't much care what becomes of your ma and pa."

"Sheriff?"

Slocum scowled. Sarah must not have seen Kincaid riding into town. He brushed it off. She had been mighty scared when Ethan Crain had chased her and had driven away with her folks tied to the wheels of the family's wagon. But she acted like a different person than the wanton who had made love upstairs in the saloon or who had walked right on up to Crain demanding the release of her parents.

"You must have missed him. He finished off Marcus Tennyson over by the stables."

"I heard shots. I thought it was you." Sarah swallowed hard, trying not to cry. "I worried that they might have shot you, John. I'm glad they didn't."

"We have to work quick. Do you know where Crain is or where he might have holed up with your ma and pa?" Slocum returned to where his Winchester rested on the boards. He cautiously considered the chances of reaching the wagon, if the outlaw was inside it.

Slocum was a betting man but not a foolish one. Unless he knew where Ethan Crain had gone, he wasn't going over to the wagon. Slocum almost laughed when he amended his wariness by telling himself he wasn't anything like the fearless Abe Kincaid.

"There's a good-sized building over yonder," Sarah said, pointing. "I don't know what it is, but it looks like the kind of place a man like Crain might make a stand."

The building was a large storehouse. Near the rear of several mercantile stores, Slocum decided it had once held freight from whatever source supplied Buzzard Flats. It probably held more of interest to Slocum now than it ever had. Sarah was right that this was the sort of position easily defended by Ethan Crain.

"We don't have much time," Slocum said. He didn't know how long it had been since he'd left Kincaid, but the implacable lawman wasn't going to linger long. Slocum almost expected to see the tall, emaciated man walking slowly down the main street, heading straight for the storehouse.

"John, they might all be together. I thought I heard horses a few minutes before I found you, but I couldn't be sure."

Slocum moved along the street, keeping behind whatever cover he could find. The oxen shifted from foot to foot as they stood in front of the wagon. They were so docile that Slocum reckoned the outlaws had abandoned them and gone on, probably into the storehouse. But he wished he could be sure.

"I'll go find out. You stay here. You understand what I'm saying? No heroics."

"John, please, I don't know what got into me facing down Ethan Crain the way I did. I know it was wrong, but I . . . I couldn't help myself. It was as if I were someone else." Sarah started to launch into more explanation, but Slocum was already hurrying across the street, crouched over to present the smallest target possible if he was wrong. The outlaws might be in the back of the wagon, no matter what he thought.

Slocum dived and landed hard, skidding in the dirt under the wagon. He poked the muzzle of the Winchester straight up, ready to fire through the bed if he heard any sounds. That was dangerous and might injure or kill the very people he was trying to rescue, but Slocum wanted to stay alive. Sarah needed help getting back to the wagon train, he told himself, and there wasn't much he could do for the Stoners if he let the outlaws kill him.

Even Kincaid might not be much of an answer, as single-minded as the lawman was about bringing the Tennyson gang to deadly justice.

Slocum heard nothing over his head. The oxen stirred and lowed a mite, causing the wagon to roll against its brake. Slocum pressed his eye against the splintery bottom and found a hole big enough to peer through. He worked his way along cracks in the lumber until he satisfied himself nobody hid in the wagon bed.

Motioning to Sarah, he got the woman across the street and under the wagon with him.

"Listen real careful," he told her. "I want you to get my horse and be ready to ride on out of here with your folks, if I can get them out of the storehouse in one piece."

"John, what about you?" Real concern colored her words.

"I might be able to take a few of the Tennysons' horses, if they won't be needing them." Slocum heard the distant neighing of horses from inside the storehouse and knew the desperados had holed up there. Or at least one had.

Ethan Crain was there with his prisoners, Slocum guessed. What about Jeb Tennyson? Slocum had to act as if the second outlaw waited inside, too. Anything else would mean he'd get careless and leave his back exposed. Men like the Tennysons weren't too polite about asking before shooting a fellow down.

"How will I know when to come?" asked Sarah.

"You'll know. Just keep a sharp eye out and don't be gulled by any trick the Tennysons might use."

"All right," Sarah said doubtfully. She ran back across the street and made for wherever she had tied up the Appaloosa. Slocum took a deep breath as he watched her go. She was one lovely woman, and he tried to tell himself he'd be doing this for her parents even if she were the ugliest crone west of the Mississippi.

He might be, but Slocum wasn't enough of a gambling man to put much money on that notion. He rolled from under the wagon and started for the storehouse, trying to see where sentries might be posted. With only two of the gang left, they'd have a hard time keeping watch all around. As far as Slocum could tell, nobody stood watch.

That made it easier for him to get close to the storehouse, even if he couldn't get inside. He pressed his face against the splintery wall, as he had done under the wagon. This time he was rewarded with a view of Immanuel Stoner's back. The man was trussed up and dumped onto a pile of burlap bags.

"Stoner," Slocum hissed, trying to get the man's attention. Stoner stirred but didn't respond. Slocum didn't want to call out too loudly or he'd draw unwanted attention.

He moved a few feet and got a better look at the captive man. Stoner wasn't in any condition to answer. Ethan Crain had tied him so that his ankles were pulled up close to his butt, a loop of rope around both ankles and neck. If Stoner tried lowering his legs, he would strangle himself.

Slocum stood and tried to get a better look inside the huge outbuilding. Distant voices drifted to him, men's voices. Arguing something fierce. Slocum knew this was his chance. If he wanted to get Stoner and his wife free, he'd have to do it while Jeb Tennyson argued with his cousin. Waiting too long would give them back the upper hand.

"They don't know I'm coming," Slocum muttered. He walked quickly to the main doors and gently tried to open them. They were barred on the inside. Slocum kept walking, hunting for a way inside. He found it in an unlikely spot.

At the far side of the storehouse some animal had burrowed under the wall to get inside. It might have been a large rabbit or a medium-sized dog. Slocum didn't much care. It gave him a place to start. He leaned his rifle against the wall and sized up the chore ahead. Scooping out the soft dirt, he quickly enlarged the hole enough to slide through on his back. Shoulders brushing the sides of his tunnel, Slocum squirmed like a snake and managed to come up inside the storehouse in a dark, cramped space.

Banging about for a few seconds, Slocum subsided. He paused to listen. If he had drawn attention to himself, he was a goner.

"What's that, Jeb? I heard somethin'. Came from back yonder."

"Dammit, you're jumping at shadows," his cousin snapped. "We got real trouble. I don't know what's happened to Mark. I went a 'lookin' for him, and he was nowhere to be seen. I shouted and hollered and did what I could, but I think that cowboy with those homesteaders might have got him."

"Nobody gets the best of Mark. He's the damnedest, fastest gun in all of Dakota Territory. 'Cept maybe for you, Jeb," Ethan Crain said quickly.

The two went on arguing while Slocum got his feet up under him. He was doubled over in a small shed without any doors. Standing slowly, Slocum pushed up the lid on a supply bin enough to peer into the dim interior. A kerosene lamp blazed across the storehouse, shedding enough light to see. Other than this, the entire building was draped in obscuring shadow.

Not wanting to leave his haven until he had located Lottie Stoner, Slocum studied every inch of his surroundings. He saw Immanuel Stoner across the empty room, struggling weakly and making choking sounds. Slocum knew the sodbuster wouldn't last much longer. His legs would knot up and weaken, and then he'd find it impossible to keep from strangling himself.

This added urgency to getting him away from the Tennysons, but Slocum wasn't going to die in the attempt.

"Immanuel," came a choked whisper. "Can you roll onto your side? Will that help?"

Slocum recognized Lottie's voice immediately. He couldn't see her, but she had to be tied up just a few feet beyond her husband. Creeping from the storage bin, Slocum crawled across the floor toward the captives. Ethan Crain and his cousin continued to argue over what might have happened to the third member of their family.

Slocum listened with half an ear, amused that they hadn't thought that it might be the law coming down on them. Abe Kincaid and the Tennyson gang had crossed paths before. That much was apparent from the way Kincaid turned killing Marcus Tennyson into a personal matter. Slocum had seen some cold deeds in his day but cutting the finger off a dead

108 JAKE LOGAN

man to steal a ring was about the most chilling.

The thought crossed his mind that Tennyson might have done something similar to get the ring in the first place.

"Mr. Slocum!"

"Hush," he whispered to Lottie Stoner. "Don't draw their attention. If shooting starts, there's no way you or your husband will get out of this alive." Slocum didn't want to add that he'd be the first to get a gut full of lead.

"Is Sarah all right?" asked the anxious mother.

"She's just fine and is waiting outside to help us get away." Slocum swung around and put his back against the storehouse's outer wall. He pulled his knife out and made short work of the ropes binding Lottie Stoner's hands behind her back. He sawed through the heavier lariat used on her feet but saw immediately that she wouldn't be walking for a few minutes.

The woman's feet had swollen from having the circulation cut off for so long.

"Rub your ankles as hard as you can. When you think you can walk, let me know." Slocum made his way to Immanuel Stoner and severed the taut rope slowly strangling the man. Stoner's legs crashed onto the pile of burlap, kicking up a cloud of dust. The man was blue in the face from strangulation. If Slocum hadn't come when he had, the man wouldn't have lasted another five minutes.

"Can you—" Slocum bit off his words and hunkered down when he heard the two outlaws stop their argument. He might have made a loud noise or Stoner himself might have alerted them. The man's grunts and choking gurgles had stopped when the killing pressure around his neck was removed.

"Did that old goat finally hang hisself?" Ethan Crain seemed to find the notion of Stoner's death funny.

"Could be. We might—Ethan, it's him. That cowboy."

Slocum fumbled for his Colt Navy, but the outlaws had their six-shooters out and blazing before he could draw. The room filled with white smoke and leaden death. All Slocum could do was roll and try to keep from getting ventilated until his own Colt came free.

Slocum fetched up hard against a wall, but this gave him the chance to go for his six-shooter. His heart almost exploded when he realized he had dropped his Colt Navy getting out of the line of fire. He was unarmed and at the mercy of men who didn't know the meaning of the word.

12

Slocum still held his knife. Backhanded, he threw it toward Ethan Crain. The outlaw was in no danger of having the pig-sticker do any damage but he flinched. And this was all Slocum needed to shove hard against the wall with his feet and shoulders and roll back toward Immanuel Stoner.

Scooping up his Colt Navy, Slocum fired two quick shots in the direction of Tennyson and his cousin. Jeb Tennyson got off a round but had run afoul of Crain. This was all that saved Slocum. He got a third shot, more accurate than the first two. This one caught Ethan Crain square in the belly.

"He got me," groaned the outlaw, doubling over and folding like a bad poker hand. "I'm dyin', Jeb. Don't let the son of a bitch get by with killin' me. Get him. Get him now!"

Slocum knew that his shot had wounded Ethan Crain but wasn't fatal. From the sound, the slug might have struck Crain's belt buckle, robbing it of killing power. The man wouldn't be squealing so loud if it had been too serious a wound. Slocum fired twice more, saving the last round for a killing shot. He wasn't given the chance. Both outlaws ducked behind a grain bin.

Slocum considered rescuing Immanuel Stoner, but the man wasn't in any condition to run for it. He lay moaning in pain, more dead than alive from his strangulation torture. Slocum rolled back to where Lottie Stoner cowered.

"We have to get out of here. They'll rush us any instant. I've only got one round left, and there's no time to reload."

"But Immanuel! We cannot leave him. They will kill him for certain!"

"We'll do what we can. If they haven't killed him before now, they have plans for him," Slocum said, saying whatever might convince the woman to make a getaway. Telling Sarah he had lost her father was a damned sight better than telling her he had watched both her parents die at the Tennysons' hands.

"Are you sure?" The woman's tone showed she wasn't convinced by his argument, but the need to live burned brightly in her breast. Her pale gray eyes took on more life than Slocum remembered ever seeing before.

"That bin," Slocum said, pointing. "Get into it and slip through the hole in the bottom. It'll get you outside. I have a rifle there. We can use that to rescue your husband."

Lottie Stoner didn't argue any further. She darted toward the bin, ducking and weaving better than Slocum would have given her credit for. Ethan Crain lifted his head and tried to get his hogleg around to shoot the woman, but Slocum's single remaining round blew splinters into the gunman's face. Crain vanished like a nightmare, complaining that he was again wounded.

Slocum knew better. The shot hadn't been anywhere near close enough to actually plug Crain. He sucked in his breath, then let out a loud shout to keep the outlaws from thinking too much about the number of times he'd fired. Slocum dived headfirst into the bin, hit the uneven floor, and found the hole fast. Behind him the wooden bin exploded as the Tennysons opened fire.

Even outside, there was little escape. The rotted wood walls didn't provide much sanctuary from the wildly flying lead. Slocum grabbed his Winchester and shouted for Lottie Stoner.

112   JAKE LOGAN

"Here, Mr. Slocum. Over here!"

The woman had the good sense not to stand around waiting for him. She was near the row of stores on the main street. Slocum looked around for Sarah but didn't see her. It was just as well because Jeb Tennyson poked his head around the side of the storehouse and yelled for his cousin.

Ethan Crain was slower to join in firing, but Slocum was still forced to the ground. Flat on his belly, he fired several rifle shots in the outlaws' direction, forcing them back for a few seconds. It was enough for him to sprint to join Lottie Stoner.

"Where do we go?"

"I thought Sarah was going to be here with a horse," Slocum said. He didn't see hide nor hair of the lovely young woman. It might be for the best because the Tennyson gang insisted on keeping the lead singing through the air. They were terrible shots but sooner or later they would hit something if they fired enough times.

"We can't leave Immanuel in there. They will do terrible things to him." A catch came to Mrs. Stoner's voice. "You weren't there, Mr. Slocum. They told us what they were going to do. It was awful."

"I'm sure it was," Slocum said, calculating his odds for getting away without being drilled a dozen times. "We might have an ally against them."

"Sarah can't—"

"Not Sarah. A lawman rode into town and killed Mark Tennyson. Abe Kincaid is about the fastest draw I ever saw," Slocum said truthfully. When he had seen Kincaid slap leather, he evaluated his own chances against the Buzzard Flats lawman. Slocum was good. Kincaid was about the best. Not even John Wesley Hardin had such blinding speed and deadly accuracy.

"Where is this lawman?" Mrs. Stoner asked. "We can surely use a bit of friendly company about now."

A new flight of bullets ripped and tore at the walls around them, forcing both Slocum and Lottie Stoner back toward the main street. Slocum had hoped to steal the Tennysons'

Slocum kept pushing the woman under the flooring until they got out the side. Both were coated with mud, and Slocum was afraid his rifle muzzle had taken on a gob of dirt. It would take a few seconds for him to check—and it was time they didn't have. The tinder-dry store was burning hotly just a few feet away.

"Keep crawling. Under this store," he urged, guiding Mrs. Stoner toward the next store. By the time they had wiggled and squirmed under three stores, Slocum poked up his head and took the lay of the land. It was about as bad as he had expected.

Two stores blazed brightly, but the adjoining stores somehow escaped a fiery fate. What bothered him most was Jeb Tennyson. The outlaw strutted around in the street, a six-shooter in either hand. He fired randomly, not caring if he hit anything.

"Come on out and take your medicine, cowboy!" the outlaw bellowed. "And bring the little lady with you. I surely do have a hankering to sample what she's been hidin' under that long skirt of hers."

"I'll kill him with my bare hands," raged Lottie Stoner. This was the most emotion Slocum had seen in the woman. He had thought her a quiet little mouse, hidden in her husband's ample shadow. The fire he prized so in the woman's daughter had been inherited honestly.

"Let me get him." Slocum watched Tennyson through a rippling curtain of heat from the burning buildings. He and Lottie Stoner were in no danger from the fire, but the Tennysons were another matter. Slocum brought his rifle to his shoulder, knowing how hard this shot would be. He squeezed the trigger smoothly.

The explosion knocked him staggering.

"Mr. Slocum, are you all right? What happened?"

"Damnation," Slocum said. "Excuse me, Mrs. Stoner." Slocum shook his head until it cleared. Turning the rifle around he saw that his worst fear had happened. The old cartridge he had found in Sheriff Kincaid's office had misfired. The gunpowder hadn't discharged fully, causing the bullet to

116   JAKE LOGAN

lodge in the barrel and gas to vent through the breech. It would take an hour's work to ream out the lead bullet, repair the firing chamber and get the weapon into usable condition.

Slocum was out of ammo for his Colt Navy, and now the Winchester was worthless.

"We have to keep moving," Slocum told the woman. "If we get out of town, we can—"

"I won't leave Immanuel!"

"You want him to catch you?" Slocum pointed in Jeb Tennyson's direction. Slocum wasn't sure if the outlaw had heard the misfire or if he simply walked along looking for them. Jeb Tennyson let out a whoop worthy of any Cheyenne brave and began firing. His bullets winged through the shimmer of heat and caused his aim to be off.

Slocum grabbed Lottie Stoner's arm and dragged her into the next street over from the burning buildings. It was more an alley than a street, but Slocum knew they wouldn't get ten feet before Tennyson caught up with them. He plunged into a store and fell through the floor. Pulling his foot free, he kept tugging at her until the woman followed.

They crouched behind a pile of boards, Slocum peering out to see if Tennyson was after them. He breathed a mite easier when he didn't see the outlaw.

"What do you intend to do, Mr. Slocum? Run all day?"

"Seems to me that's all your husband has ever done," Slocum said, not feeling too inclined to accept reproach. He had rescued her and that ought to be enough for the moment.

"Where is Sarah?"

"I told her to get out of town. We'll have to find her once we get away from here." Slocum poked his head up again and a shiver climbed his spine. Jeb Tennyson hadn't been able to flush them out with fire and bullets. He had hit upon a new tactic sure to work.

The outlaws pulled Immanuel Stoner into the middle of the street and dumped him facedown for anyone caring to look. Ethan Crain hobbled along, clutching his belly. Slocum wished he had put another round into the son of a bitch. Crain was wounded but still capable of devilment.

"You out there, cowboy? How about you, Miz Stoner? You want to see what we can do?" Jeb Tennyson said something to Ethan Crain, who brayed like a donkey.

Slocum cursed under his breath when he saw Crain hold up a thick-bladed hunting knife—the one Slocum had carried for years. The outlaw let the sunlight glint off the blade before he stabbed downward with it. Slocum had seen his share of torture, and blood didn't bother him too much, even when it was his own, but he had to keep Mrs. Stoner from seeing what the outlaws did to her husband.

She tried to push up and look, but he held her back. At this distance they couldn't hear Immanuel Stoner's feeble moans, but from the way the man twitched and kicked impotently he was hurting bad. Ethan Crain kept cutting and slicing, tossing parts away. Slocum didn't know if this was mostly theatrics or if vital parts of Immanuel Stoner's body were being hacked off.

"I want to see, Mr. Slocum." His strong grip prevented Lottie Stoner from witnessing what he did.

"We got to get out of Buzzard Flats and find Sarah. She'll be worrying over us if we don't get away real quick." Slocum cast one last look at the middle of the street to see how the outlaws brutalized their prisoner. Slocum vowed to get both men.

And where the hell was Abe Kincaid? The man had killed Marcus Tennyson and then vanished. Of all the things Slocum might think of the sheriff, coward wasn't one. He had seen the way Kincaid walked through a rain of bullets to trap his quarry. But what had become of the man? Slocum hated to consider it, but the outlaws might have dry-gulched him, though when was something of a poser. Slocum had been given only a few short minutes to attack the Tennyson gang, and he had found the two survivors inside the storehouse. It hardly seemed likely they had gunned down Abe Kincaid.

"You're not running out on him, are you?" Lottie Stoner stood her ground, hands on hips. She was small but as resolute as any granite spire Slocum had ever seen.

Slocum said, "I'll get him away from them," hating to admit that he might be returning a corpse to the woman for burial.

They ducked out the back of the ruined store and started walking toward the outskirts of town, taking advantage of whatever cover they could find along the way.

13

"You didn't have *any* ammunition?" Sarah Stoner cried in surprise. She looked from Slocum to her mother and back. The woman shook her head and tried to say something more, then couldn't.

"Why didn't you tell me back in town?" demanded Lottie Stoner. "I had a right to know. You were shooting left and right in the storehouse like some battle in the war, then you upped and stopped. I thought you were running like some coward because you'd had enough."

Slocum seethed that the woman could think for an instant that he might be a yellowbelly but kept his anger in check. They had walked from Buzzard Flats, dodging through stands of juniper and lodgepole pine, finding the forest paths poorly travelled and less likely to be found by the Tennysons. Slocum's tactics had worked, and they had gotten five miles from town without being seen before he cut back to the main road, such as it was, to hunt for Sarah's tracks.

He had found the Appaloosa's hoofprints quickly. It had taken another two hours to find where Sarah had camped. He ignored the two women's demands for him to explain what was going on and rummaged through his saddlebags until he got his spare ammunition for the Colt Navy. Sitting and reloading, he felt better. Only when he had finished did he look up at them. His expression silenced them.

"I didn't want to leave your pa—Mr. Stoner—back there. I know what men like those owlhoots can do. But getting Mrs. Stoner away was more important." He didn't bother adding that it was also possible. Tackling the Tennysons with only his bare hands was nothing less than a suicide mission.

"John, we didn't mean to criticize. If you'd only tell us what you intended, we'd both have agreed." Sarah sounded sincere but Slocum knew better. She resented him sending her out of town on his horse, and Mrs. Stoner resented him leaving Immanuel behind.

Slocum had to admit Sarah probably thought poorly of him for leaving her pa, too.

"I have to get my gear out if I'm going to fix the rifle." He was a good shade tree gunsmith, but he had only a few tools with him. The barrel might require reboring, something beyond his ability without a lot more tools.

The thought intruded on his bleak musing that he might find the equipment needed in Buzzard Flats. Much of the town looked as if the inhabitants had simply stepped out front of their stores, mounted and ridden off without bothering to take their belongings with them. The disrepair showed more how badly constructed the buildings had been than what was buried under them.

But any such gunsmithing tools were on the far side of Jeb Tennyson and his cousin—and their six-shooters.

He rolled the cylinder in his Colt to be sure it hadn't taken any damage. It sounded and felt right to him. He tucked it back into his cross-draw holster and tried to decide what he wanted to do.

"I'll go back after him in a few hours," Slocum said, seeing that the sun was dipping low. "The Tennysons will get a bit drunker and might not pay much attention in the dark. I can cut them down and—"

"There's been too much killing, Mr. Slocum. I want you

to capture those awful men and take them to this sheriff you keep mentioning."

"Yes, John, where is he? You told me he had killed Mark Tennyson. I can't imagine any lawman simply turning his back when these ruffians are running amok." Sarah seemed genuinely irate that Abe Kincaid had failed her, and she had never even set eyes on the man.

"I'll do what it takes to get your pa free," Slocum said. "I might not have to do much, though. I'm sure Kincaid isn't the kind to give up on a job and go home with it unfinished." Slocum remembered the set to the man's thin shoulders, the way he had defied death repeatedly simply to get close to Marcus Tennyson. Of all the things Kincaid might be, a quitter wasn't one.

"You mean he might already have rescued Father?" Hope flared on Sarah's exquisite features. For this moment anything Slocum had gone through was worth it.

"Depending on him will be a mistake," Mrs. Stoner said harshly. "You must fetch Immanuel, to be sure he isn't hurt further."

Slocum didn't say anything about Stoner's condition. It would take a strong man to survive the torture Ethan Crain was meting out when Slocum had left Buzzard Flats.

"What can we do to help?" Sarah meant one thing, Slocum intended another and told her.

"You and your ma will stay put. If I can get your pa, I will. Otherwise—" Slocum stopped talking and reconsidered what he was saying. The women were feisty. If he didn't sound confident enough on getting the family's patriarch free, they'd follow him and he'd have to watch out for more than his own back.

He cleared his throat and said, "I'll get him, but I need to know where you'll be. So you two stay camped here. There's a stream down yonder, and the little food that was in my saddlebags will serve you well enough until we can get to your larder."

"You will wait until complete darkness?" asked Mrs. Stoner.

Slocum knew it was as dark now as it was likely to. The ring of mountains surrounding this gentle-appearing valley cut off the sun early in the day. All Slocum really needed to consider was how long Stoner was likely to survive his torment at the outlaws' hands.

Slocum heaved himself to his feet. The answer to that question was simple. The odds were against Stoner still being alive. He had almost strangled earlier. Crain's use of Slocum's own hunting knife would have bled the man something fierce.

"I'll see what I can do now. Take this," Slocum said, handing Sarah his spare Colt. "It's loaded, and you know how to use it. Just don't go shooting shadows until you know what's in them." He didn't cotton much to coming back and having her fill him full of his own lead.

"Hurry back, John." Sarah started to give him a kiss, but her mother cleared her throat and stopped the young woman. She reached out and squeezed his arm, promising more than the older woman ever would have for a safe return.

Slocum tipped his hat in Mrs. Stoner's direction, then swung into the saddle. He walked his Appaloosa slowly back toward Buzzard Flats, wondering what the hell he was going to do. Immanuel Stoner had to be dead, unless Abe Kincaid had come to his rescue. But there hadn't been any gunfire echoing after him as he and Lottie Stoner had left town.

What had happened to the Buzzard Flats' sheriff? Slocum wanted to find Kincaid and ask, almost as much as he wanted to get out of this valley and return to Ben Carter's wagon train. Things hadn't been great with many of the sodbusters in the train, but life had been a danged sight better than having a Cheyenne war party after him and letting the Tennyson gang fill him with holes and torture the Stoners.

Nearing the dark, silent town, Slocum dismounted and found a small stand of scrub oak to hide his horse. He checked his Colt one last time, then worked his way back into Buzzard Flats.

His nose began to wrinkle from the smell of charred wood. Slocum went toward the burned-out stores where he and Lottie Stoner had hidden only a few hours earlier. Some embers glowed a dull cherry red, and smoke still rose in fitful, curling columns. Other than this, Slocum found no evidence anyone had been in Buzzard Flats any time during the past few months.

Cautiously entering the street, he made his way to the spot where Ethan Crain had so brutally tortured Immanuel Stoner. Two deep ruts in the dirt showed where the sodbuster had been dragged away. Slocum followed the twin furrows back toward the storehouse, then stopped and stared.

The Tennysons had hoisted Stoner up on the studier of the storehouse doors and nailed him there. Slocum resisted the urge to rush to the crucified man, knowing this was probably a trap. Circling the area, he hunted for any sign that the two killers were waiting for him. He found nothing.

Slocum spun, his six-shooter lifting when he heard a low moan. He hardly believed it possible, but Stoner was still alive. The man kicked weakly, banging his head against the door.

"Help me," came the feeble plea. "Can't go on much longer. Help me."

Slocum sought the outlaws' horses and didn't find them. He looked high and low for any sign that what remained of the Tennyson gang was even in Buzzard Flats and couldn't unearth any spoor. And of Abe Kincaid he saw nothing.

"Here goes nothing," Slocum said, sliding his pistol back into his holster. He went to the man and tried to figure out what to do first. Slocum grabbed the handle of his hunting knife, shoved hard into the wood between Stoner's legs. Wiggling it back and forth, Slocum pulled it free, only to have the man sag down hard.

Slocum worked fast then, prying the nails from Stoner's feet and then his wrists. The sodbuster fell heavily, knocking Slocum to the ground. Slocum rolled him over and lay for a moment, waiting for some reaction. There wasn't any.

"Have they left town?" Slocum asked softly.

"Hours ago, days ago," moaned Stoner. "I hurt so bad. Help me."

"I'll be back for you. There's no way I can move you without killing you," Slocum said.

"Lottie," sobbed the man. "Is she safe?"

Slocum didn't bother answering. Stoner had passed out from the pain. Slocum tucked his knife back into its sheath and then went hunting for the Tennysons. Nowhere in Buzzard Flats did he find them—or any trace of them. More angry than pleased, Slocum went to the stables where Kincaid had cut down Marcus Tennyson. Slocum half expected for the outlaw to be where he had died, but he wasn't that startled to find only dried blood in the dirt.

Tennyson's body was gone, as were his brother Jeb and cousin Ethan.

"Did you spook 'em so bad they took off running?" Slocum said aloud, as if Kincaid would answer. The sheriff must have run them out of Buzzard Flats. This was the only explanation that made any sense, although Slocum hadn't heard any gunfire.

He returned to Stoner's side. The man breathed in slow, quick gasps. Doing what he could for him, Slocum knew Immanuel Stoner was in no condition to travel. He needed round-the-clock nursing. With the Tennysons gone, it might not be much of a risk bringing Sarah and Lottie Stoner back.

About all Slocum knew was that if he didn't do something quick, Stoner wasn't going to survive. The man had a toughness that Slocum wouldn't have guessed to be there. Even steel had a breaking point, though, and Stoner approached his quickly.

Slocum returned to his horse and galloped back to the women. Lottie Stoner sat beside a small fire they had started. He shook his head. He hadn't told them not to make a campfire, but they should have known better. Dismounting Slocum started for the woman when he heard the dull click of a six-shooter cocking.

He went into a crouch and got his Colt Navy out and aimed behind him.

"John!" came Sarah's startled voice. "It's you!"

He relaxed and stood, putting his six-shooter back into his holster. "I told you not to shoot me when I got back."

"We set a trap. I . . . we, oh, never mind. Did you find Father?"

Slocum saw that the shape he had mistaken for Lottie Stoner was a bush crammed into the woman's blouse and propped up near the tiny fire. Behind Sarah moved a dark shadow that Slocum figured to be Lottie. She had risked immodesty to bait a trap, hoping to catch the Tennysons.

"We have to get back into Buzzard Flats right away." Slocum quickly told them what he had found—and what he hadn't.

"It'll be safe?" asked Sarah as her mother retrieved her blouse and quickly dressed.

"There's no moving your pa. He's cut up bad." Slocum didn't burden the women with how he had found Immanuel Stoner. His injuries would be hard enough to accept. "If he makes it, it'll be a miracle."

"Father has a way of making such things happen," Sarah said, trying to sound unconcerned. "He is a hard man and demands the best of everyone, including himself. But he can do whatever's necessary."

"I am ready, Mr. Slocum. There is no time to waste, if what you say is right." Lottie Stoner stood primly beside him, arms crossed and waiting impatiently to get back to town and her husband.

Slocum let the women ride his Appaloosa while he walked briskly beside. They didn't speak much even after they got to Stoner. Lottie Stoner immediately began nursing her husband, but after Sarah had boiled water and they had the man's wounds cleaned and bandaged, she chased her daughter off.

"What else can I do?" Sarah asked Slocum. She stared at her mother sitting quietly beside her father. Slocum knew how useless she felt, but there was nothing much she could do. Only her father's constitution and her mother's resolve would prevail now.

"We ought to get the wagons loaded. When your pa can be moved, we should be ready."

Sarah nodded and walked beside him, looking back toward her parents more than where she was going. They reached the damaged wagon. Slocum crawled under and examined the axle. David Stoner and his father hadn't done a good job replacing the broken axle, and Slocum saw no way of keeping their handiwork intact for the trip back to the wagon train.

"We'll have to load what we can into the other wagon," he told the young woman. Sarah chewed on her lower lip and nodded, not really listening.

Slocum crawled from under the wagon and jumped onto the back, sitting beside her.

"It's been hell, I know, but we can get out of here and rejoin the wagon train. Then everything will be just fine."

"He might die, John. I never thought of that before. My father might die from what those terrible men did." She turned her face toward his. The pale light from the moon turned her skin to a warm, living marble. "You saw them doing it, didn't you?"

"I couldn't stop them," Slocum said, the memory eating at his guts.

"It's all right, John. I understand. I understand everything."

And then Sarah kissed him. Gently at first, then harder, with more passion. She kissed and he returned it. He wrapped his arms around her and drew her closer, relishing the feel of her soft body next to his. Slocum leaned back and they lay down in the hard wagon bed.

Fumbling behind her, Sarah pulled blankets and other padding around for them to lie on. Somehow, as she moved, her blouse came unbuttoned. The moon shining down was dim inside the wagon, but Slocum saw the way the light danced on Sarah's breasts, turning them into something so delectable he couldn't resist.

He pulled her blouse open all the way and buried his face between the luscious mounds of flesh. His tongue licked and teased, and his teeth bit lightly. Sarah moaned softly and went limp in his arms. Slocum kept up his oral assault, working slowly up the steep slopes of her left breast. His tongue pressed down on the hard, pink button he found. Her heart pounded so hard he felt every beat.

"John, wait, no, we can't. My ma isn't far off."

"She's occupied," Slocum said. "And you ought to be, too." He gave her as much to keep her mind engrossed as he could.

His tongue lashed out and batted about the taut nubbin of nipple, then slowly raked the side of the flesh beneath with his tongue. He left behind a trail that turned to liquid silver in the moonlight.

He had been giving her reason to stay. Now Sarah gave him reason to continue. Her hand worked between his belly and his belt, moving ever lower until her fingertips tickled his balls. She cupped her hand and stroked, but it wasn't enough for Slocum. He quickly undid his gunbelt and jeans and moved closer so his hardening length pressed firmly into the circle of her hand.

Sarah began stroking up and down gently. Then as her own passion mounted, she gripped firmly and pulled him even closer. Slocum grunted as he positioned himself on his knees between the gorgeous young woman's spread thighs.

"Now, John. Don't hold back. I need you. I need to forget, just for a moment."

Sarah's eyes shone like limpid pools without bottom. Slocum knew what she needed and why. This was more than sex for her. Sarah Stoner needed to forget, if only for a few precious minutes, the terrible things that had befallen her family. And Slocum wasn't going to deny her that release.

His hands stroked along the insides of her white thighs, parting them a bit more. He brushed her skirts out of the way and touched the soft, fleecy triangle between her legs. Sarah closed her eyes and sighed deeply. Slocum's finger intruded on her and moved about in unhurried circles. Every movement made Sarah's breath come a mite faster and her body to tremble that much more.

When her rear end raised off the wagon bed and she tried shoving herself down harder onto his hand, Slocum knew he couldn't resist her any longer. She was ready, and so was he. The pressures building deep in his balls felt like a volcano ready to erupt. Sliding forward, his blood-engorged tip touched her most delicate flesh.

Then he plunged forward so hard Sarah shrieked. Her legs came up and locked around his waist. Even if he had wanted to, she wasn't going to let him leave. All around his hidden length he felt warm female flesh clenching, teasing, tormenting. The pressures he had felt before multiplied now until he was hard-pressed to keep from spilling his seed like a young buck with his first woman.

"I need it like that, John. Hard. Fast. Set me on fire inside."

Sarah's fingers clawed at his arms and back, pulling him to her even harder than before. He broke free and withdrew until only the cap of his manhood remained hidden. Then he lost all control.

He began slamming forward, trying to tear her apart. He needed the release from death and Buzzard Flats and the Tennysons as much as Sarah. Lost in the pleasures they shared, they rocked and groaned and merged. Slocum exploded and shot forth his load. Sarah arched her back as her own desires burst within her body.

Sarah shuddered once, twice, a third time and then sagged limply. Slocum had sweat profusely during the violent lovemaking and tried to shake himself off before lying beside her. She wouldn't let him take the time. Sarah wanted him just the way he was. He put his arm around the young woman's shoulders and held her close.

For a long time she didn't speak, then Sarah said, "I don't know how to thank you for all you've done, John. You could have left us here in this forsaken town and returned to the wagon train."

"No," Slocum said. "I couldn't have done that." He kissed her and soon he was showing her again what they both would have missed had he neglected his duty.

14

"He had a bad night, didn't he?" Slocum asked Sarah of her father. She didn't look Slocum in the eye, as if she remembered what they had been doing in the family wagon while her mother tended the injured man. Slocum wasn't going to feel any guilt about their night together. Life went on, and if Immanuel Stoner lived, it would be his own doing. They had done everything possible for him, and Lottie Stoner hadn't done anything more than hold his hand for hours.

If he died, Stoner's murder was just one more crime added to the long list dogging the Tennysons' trail.

"Ma says he recognized her when he came to around midnight, but he's burning up with fever. I've looked around for herbs to bring down the fever but nothing's the same around here. I'm used to what grows wild in Missouri, not Wyoming." Sarah moved away from him, eyes on the ground. Slocum considered stopping her, telling her that she was doing all that anyone could.

Why he held back comforting her, he wasn't sure.

"We're going to have to make some hard decisions on what gets loaded into your second wagon and what gets left behind. I know everything is precious, but there's not as many of you now." Slocum was getting antsy just standing around, wanting action and not knowing what else to say about David Stoner, about Immanuel Stoner, about their troubles. Mostly, he worried that the Tennyson gang, such as it was now that Mark Tennyson was dead, might return to Buzzard Flats for more of their poisonous devilment. Slocum reckoned that Kincaid had chased them out, but he was one man against two.

No matter how determined the sheriff might be, the Tennysons had been successful thieves for a long time. Slocum didn't know what they'd been doing since they rustled the entire herd in his care, but it sure as hell wasn't county quilting bees. They were cold-blooded killers—and worse. They enjoyed watching their victims beg before they slaughtered them.

"I can go through the goods already out of the main wagon," Sarah said. She sounded as weak as if she stood a mile off, and Slocum guessed that was where her thoughts were.

"That's something only you can do. Your ma's not going to leave your pa's side. I want to scout around and see if I can find what happened to the Tennysons." Slocum tried to decide which direction the cousins might have ridden. Without a careful search of the countryside, there wasn't any way he could find them. Ethan Crain and Jeb Tennyson might have ridden right by him as he returned to Buzzard Flats.

Or they might have hightailed it in any other direction. Slocum knew next to nothing about the lay of the land, except the parts of the valley he had already traversed.

He scratched his head, remembering the strange events he had been witness to, getting into Buzzard Flats. The Cheyennes had simply given up their chase when he had routed the red rock butte. Trails of light freight wagons and footprints that shouldn't have lasted days, much less years. The way Sarah acted in the saloon and after was completely unlike her. And there had been the fresh blood on a carriage wrecked years earlier.

"Skeleton," mumbled Slocum, remembering the horse's sun-bleached carcass. The horse pulling the buggy had been reduced to white bones, long burned by Wyoming's hot summer sun and frozen by long, cold winters.

"What's that, John?" Sarah turned and stared at him, as if he had sprouted wings and had started flying away.

"Nothing. I might get lucky and find the town's sheriff. He didn't seem the kind of lawman to give up easily. I figure Kincaid's responsible for chasing them off. That's the only thing that makes any sense."

"What sense is there in calling him sheriff?" demanded Sarah. "He's sheriff of *this* horrid place?" She gestured, her sweeping arm taking in every tumbledown shack in Buzzard Flats.

"Didn't have much chance to ask Sheriff Kincaid any questions. We were both occupied with other concerns." But Slocum's curiosity was burning him up inside. If Kincaid wasn't sheriff of this empty town, then he had to be related to the former sheriff. Slocum remembered how Kincaid had touched his vest, just about where a badge would be pinned, and how he acted.

Lawmen viewed the world differently from ordinary citizens. Slocum had seen enough marshals, sheriffs, and rangers in his day to know one when he saw one. There was the walk, the set to the chin, the steely glint in the eye expecting the worst from every man and woman.

"I hope he gets them," Sarah said, still averting her eyes. "I'd better see if Ma needs help. She's not sleeping or even eating much. All she does is stare at him, as if she can will him to get better." For the first time, Sarah turned and stared at him. Her chocolate eyes brimmed with unshed tears.

Slocum reached out and rested his hand on the woman's shoulder. He said gently, "Maybe she can. There's got to be more than medicine in healing."

Sarah smiled wanly and hurried off. Slocum watched as she offered her mother some of the dried provisions they had found in the broken-down wagon. Lottie Stoner pushed the food away, as if she couldn't be bothered with such commonplace details.

Turning from the women, Slocum mounted his Appaloosa and rode slowly from Buzzard Flats. As he rode, he thought on how easy it would be to keep going, never to return. He shook himself hard, like a dog climbing out of a stock tank. That was an unworthy thought, and he had no idea why it had entered his head. They had been through much together, and Slocum wasn't about to desert them now. David Stoner had been murdered, and Immanuel Stoner wasn't likely to make it much longer. Sarah and her mother needed Slocum's help more than ever.

Slocum fumbled in his vest and pulled out a rolling paper and a bag of fixings. The paper had seen better days, being soaked and dried more times than Slocum cared to think on. He opened the bag and doled out the tobacco as if he were a miser at payday. Pulling the string with his teeth, he put the flattened pouch back in his vest pocket and tended to the rolling.

Smoking as he hunted for the Tennysons might not be the smartest course of action, but he needed the relaxing flow of smoke into his lungs. Ever since entering this valley—Buzzard Flats—he had been plagued with foggy thinking. It was as if the town itself beclouded his mind. Slocum had seen Sarah act out of character, and he had done things himself that defied explanation.

For some reason, he kept going back to Buzzard Flats, almost as if he was made of iron and the deserted town was a lodestone.

Slocum snorted and finished his smoke. "Seems I'm not the only one thinking there's something singular in Buzzard Flats. Kincaid and the Tennysons don't seem free to pass it by, either."

Somehow, that notion chilled him.

Slocum rode in a wide circle around the town, hunting for recent hoofprints. It took almost an hour before he came across a faint trail leading from Buzzard Flats. Dismounting, Slocum studied them carefully, then followed the trail on foot for several hundred yards until he was sure he wasn't following some old trail. The wind had partly obscured the hoofprints, but Slocum finally found a new pile of horse dung, still warm enough to draw flies.

"So you're going back out the canyon," Slocum said, eyes rising to the red butte marking the entrance to the canyon leading in the direction of the Cheyenne war party. The Tennysons might be riding into the teeth of a trap laid by the Indians, but Slocum doubted it. The Cheyenne war chief wouldn't camp at the end of the canyon, waiting for a victim to ride out. The cavalry probably hounded the renegades. They would have moved on north, out of the canyon and leaving a clear path for the fleeing outlaws.

"You're going to be mine," Slocum vowed. He mounted and put his heels into the Appaloosa's flanks. The horse responded well, and he kept up a rapid pace for almost an hour. Then Slocum began varying the horse's gait to get even more distance from it. He doubted the Tennysons were making this good a time, but they were far ahead of him.

And before long Slocum saw the hoofprints of a third horse along the trail. He smiled crookedly, knowing that the two surviving gang members had company. Deadly company. Who else but Abe Kincaid would be out here?

Slocum began worrying that he would ride over the outlaws as they rested. By sundown he was worrying that he would miss them entirely. There wasn't any sign of riders ahead, and he was sure he hadn't gone past them. He didn't credit the Tennysons with the sense God gave a goose, but they had dodged the law for years. Either luck or their stark viciousness stood them in good stead.

Slocum found a rise and studied the terrain ahead, seeing a shortcut to the butte marking the way out of the valley. If the riders followed the land's contours, he could head them off. Slocum took a deep breath. There were a whole load of "ifs" thrown into this plan. The Tennysons couldn't be too far ahead. He had ridden faster than chain lightning with a link cut, and the Tennysons looked to be moseying along with little worry about being followed.

This set Slocum to thinking harder. If Kincaid had run them out of Buzzard Flats, they'd still be racing the wind to escape,

134   JAKE LOGAN

but they were walking along as peaceful as you please. And the third set of hoofprints showed Kincaid was after them but hadn't yet caught up with the outlaws. Not much of it made any sense.

He snorted and shook his head. Not much made any sense since he'd come after the Stoners. The Cheyenne war party had him dead to rights and they had let him go. Thinking about the Indians, Slocum scanned the tops of the canyon walls and the butte for any sign of the war party. He saw nothing, but this didn't surprise him over much. The Cheyenne weren't likely to advertise their presence, if they were still around.

"Time to ride," he told his Appaloosa, patting the horse on the neck. The horse nickered softly, then got on the trail, moving even faster. Slocum liked the spotted horses for their strength and stamina. He kept up his pace until he came to the butte, then slowed and worked his way higher along rocky paths hardly big enough for a man to walk.

The going got treacherous, but Slocum thought the risk worthwhile. He needed to get above the valley floor and to a place where he could see into the canyon beyond. If he had missed the Tennysons, he had a real chase ahead. And decisions to make.

Leaving the women alone in Buzzard Flats wasn't to his liking, yet he didn't want Jeb Tennyson and his cousin getting away scot-free. They had to pay for all they had done. If Kincaid wasn't on their trail, it would be up to Slocum to be sure their lawlessness didn't go any farther than the canyon.

Slocum scanned the canyon but saw nothing to show recent passage. He would have to be on the canyon floor for real tracking. But luck was with him. A slow smile came to his lips when he saw a rider emerging from a stand of trees near a small stream back in the direction of Buzzard Flats. He had outridden the outlaws by almost ten minutes. He didn't know what kind of head start the Tennysons had, but Slocum figured this was damned good riding on his part.

Pulling his Colt Navy from its holster, he considered the best spot to ambush the outlaws. He wished he had his Winchester but knew that if wishes were ever answered, he might as well have asked for an entire cavalry detachment. Slocum walked to the brink of the rocky ledge where he stood, estimating distances. A shot of almost twenty yards was considerable for a six-shooter, but he thought he could make it if he caught the owlhoots unawares.

Slocum went over in his head the shot he needed to make. The riders would come even with him below. He would lead the first outlaw just a mite, then squeeze off the round. His Colt Navy was accurate. He might not kill the outlaw, but he would sow enough discord to make a second and third shot possible. Those rounds he dared not rush, no matter the provocation. If he could kill one outlaw, he could always run down the surviving owlhoot.

His Appaloosa neighed loudly. Slocum went to quiet the horse. He didn't want the animal giving away his trap. But gentling the horse wasn't possible. The Appaloosa reared and tried to get away. Slocum fastened its reins firmly and hurried back to the edge of the rocky overhang.

The Tennysons hadn't heard his horse. And something more caused Slocum to frown, wondering what was going on. Three horses, not two, emerged from the edge of the forest, following the faint path into the canyon.

As they drew closer, Slocum got a better look at the third horse. Mark Tennyson's body was slung over the saddle. He wondered why they hadn't buried him in Buzzard Flats— or just left him for the town's namesakes. Maybe Tennyson family blood flowed thick, or maybe they were going to turn the body in for a reward. Slocum thought anything possible when dealing with men like this.

He cocked his six-shooter and slowly tracked the leading rider. He considered switching targets when he identified Ethan Crain. He had already plugged the Tennysons' cousin and running him to earth would be easier because of his gut wound. Then Slocum realized it didn't matter. He would find whoever escaped—if anyone did.

Slocum started to squeeze off his round when the Appaloosa began neighing loudly again and kicking its hooves against the side of the butte. This distracted Slocum slightly, enough for him to realize what the horse already had. The ledge he laid belly down on was shifting under him. Slocum tried to get to his feet, but the rocky outcropping began creaking like an unoiled door hinge. Then the entire projection broke off and sent him tumbling down the hillside amid a cloud of dust and flying rock.

"Lookee there, Jeb," cried Crain. The outlaw sounded panicked. He stood in his stirrups and turned almost completely around to stare at Slocum. "It's that damned cowboy again. We ain't never gonna get free of him!"

Slocum struggled in the heap of sharp stones, trying to get his feet under him. He had been cut in a dozen places by his fall and was bleeding profusely. None of the shallow furrows in his hide was serious, but he looked as if he had fought a hard battle and lost. His eyes were filled with dust, and he worried that he wouldn't be able to see clearly enough to finish the chore he had begun.

"Get on out of here, Ethan. Meet at the usual place in a week. And good luck!"

Jeb Tennyson wheeled his horse about and whipped his pony to a gallop. He took the third horse, the one Slocum had mistakenly thought belonged to Abe Kincaid, with him. Mark Tennyson's corpse flopped and swayed as the pack horse stumbled along. Slocum waited for the body to slip free and go crashing to the ground, but Jeb Tennyson had tied his brother down too well for that.

Slocum wiped the grit from his eyes and leveled his six-shooter but didn't fire. Ethan Crain had hightailed it up the canyon. Jeb Tennyson was going back into the valley, toward Buzzard Flats. Slocum cursed his bad luck. If he had taken a tad more time to wonder why his Appaloosa was so spooked, he might have noticed the ledge getting ready to break off under him.

But this was working out just fine. Catching Ethan Crain wouldn't be too hard, not with a tiny piece of Slocum's lead still riding in his belly. And from the way Jeb Tennyson whipped his horse, it would drop dead under him within a mile. Burdened with his brother's body, Jeb couldn't get too far before Slocum overtook him.

Slocum holstered his six-gun and trudged up the treacherous, debris-strewn slope to get his horse. The Appaloosa had rested enough to make the chase easy. Slocum was almost looking forward to facing Jeb Tennyson when he cut him down. He wanted to see the fear in the outlaw's eyes before Tennyson died.

Slocum had to walk his horse back down the path. Sections of the path had joined the outcropping in its downward plunge, but Slocum took it easy, not risking too much at any point. He wanted Tennyson so bad he could taste it. To have his Appaloosa break a leg in a foolish bid for haste would be senseless.

Finally reaching the floor of the seemingly peaceful valley, Slocum hesitated for a moment to make his decision. Ethan Crain might get away if he reached the far end of the canyon. There were too many branches to hide in. But Jeb Tennyson was heading toward Buzzard Falts. Slocum felt an obligation to protect the Stoners as much as he did to end the outlaw's life.

Slocum started riding at a trot, following the broad trail left by the Tennysons' horses in the soft dirt. It wouldn't take long to overtake him, Slocum thought—and it didn't.

Before he had ridden two miles, Slocum saw that Jeb Tennyson's horse had pulled up lame. For whatever reason, Jeb Tennyson didn't throw his brother's body off the second horse and keep running. The outlaw whipped out his six-shooter and started firing.

A couple rounds whined past Slocum's head, but the range was too great for accuracy. Slocum kept riding, feeling like Kincaid in that moment. No matter what kind of fusillade Tennyson laid down, he would ride straight into the bore of the outlaw's gun.

"You going to make it easy, Tennyson?" Slocum yelled. He saw the outlaw hastily reloading his six-shooter. "Give up and I'll see that you get a fair trial somewhere." Slocum knew that

Tennyson would never give up. Slocum just wanted to make him squirm before shooting him.

"Ain't no court in Dakota Territory or anywhere else that would give my kind a fair trial. They'd string me up and *then* bring in the judge!"

Slocum didn't see too much wrong with that. It would save the time and trouble of getting a jury together. He slid from the saddle and drew his six-gun. A new flight of bullets sang noisily past him, forcing him to return fire.

Slocum's aim was better than Tennyson's, but he didn't get in a killing shot. Slocum ducked behind a fallen log and let Jeb Tennyson fill the rotting wood with lead. He snapped a couple more shots in the outlaw's direction, then made his attack. Slocum rushed forward and was rewarded with the sight of Tennyson's fear.

Jeb Tennyson turned and ran. Slocum slowed and got off a couple more shots, both missing. But they convinced Tennyson he couldn't outrun a bullet. He skidded to a halt, not ten yards from the edge of the forest where he had sought refuge. Tennyson turned, six-shooter in his hand.

"You want to try it?" called Slocum. He carefully put his Colt Navy back into its cross-draw holster. "Let's do this fair and square." Slocum widened his stance. He was less than twenty feet from the outlaw.

"You'd throw down on me?" Tennyson sounded skeptical. "All fair?"

"Do it," Slocum challenged.

Tennyson went for his gun, but Slocum was twice as fast. He cleared leather and fired—and the Colt's hammer fell on a spent chamber. Slocum hadn't counted the rounds he had fired.

A loud report echoed across the meadow as Tennyson drew and fired.

15

Slocum stood stock-still, wondering why he didn't feel the bullet ripping through him. He looked from his empty six-shooter to Jeb Tennyson. The outlaw held his own six-gun up, but it wasn't aimed in Slocum's direction—and he hadn't pulled the trigger.

"Got me," Tennyson said before he sank to his knees. He fought to lift his six-shooter but lacked the strength. He fell forward onto the ground. Slocum didn't have to check the man to know he was stone dead.

"Damnation," Abe Kincaid said from the edge of the woods. He shoved his smoking pistol back into his holster. Once more he had beaten an outlaw to the draw, though Jeb Tennyson had never known the Buzzard Flats lawman was off to one side.

"Thanks," Slocum said, starting to reload. "He would have had me dead to rights if you hadn't cut him down."

"Should'a known who killed him," Kincaid said, aggrieved. He walked slowly toward the fallen murderer and stared down at him as if force of will could resurrect Tennyson. "He died thinking you pulled the trigger on him."

"Is that so important?" Slocum was glad to still be drawing air. He finished with his Colt and tucked the six-shooter into his holster. "Dead's dead."

"Yeah," Kincaid said, as if not believing it. "But I wanted him to know *I* did him."

Slocum didn't reply, just stood and watched the lawman. He remembered how Kincaid had treated the fallen Marcus Tennyson, edging around to see the glint of a gold band on Kincaid's left ring finger. Was the sheriff going to do the same to Jeb Tennyson?

Slocum got his answer quickly. Kincaid knelt and heaved, rolling Tennyson over. The gaunt lawman slowly searched the dead outlaw, turning out every pocket to be sure nothing remained. A small roll of greenbacks was discarded, as if the money meant nothing. Tennyson even had a small pouch of gold dust. Kincaid showed no interest in this, either. For a thief, he was missing the best the dead man had to offer.

Somehow, Slocum didn't think monetary gain drove Abe Kincaid.

"What are you looking for?" Slocum asked. He didn't get an answer. The emaciated sheriff pulled off Tennyson's boots and studied the insides, as if something might be hidden there. Whatever he sought, he didn't find it.

Kincaid stood and went to catch Tennyson's horse. The lame horse hadn't gone far, even after being spooked by the gunfire. Slocum stopped beside Jeb Tennyson's body, wondering what he ought to do about the discarded money. He bent and retrieved both the greenbacks and the small pouch of gold dust. Together, the robber had less than fifty dollars on him, but it was more money than Slocum would see in two months of scouting for Benjamin Carter.

Abe Kincaid either didn't see Slocum take the money or didn't much care. Slocum thought it complete indifference on the lawman's part. Kincaid pulled Tennyson's saddlebags from behind the saddle and dumped the contents onto the ground. A sudden flash of silver caught Slocum's eye at the same time Kincaid saw it. Like a hawk swooping on its dinner, Kincaid dived on the circular piece of silver.

He rubbed what he had picked up on his vest, then turned it around and pinned on a sheriff's badge. Slocum had noticed the holes in the vest where a badge had rode for a long time and had wondered what might have become of the symbol of office. Now he knew.

Jeb Tennyson had taken it.

And Marcus Tennyson had stolen a wedding ring from Abe Kincaid.

That explained Kincaid's perseverance in hunting down the outlaws. But how had he lost his ring and badge? No one as quick as Kincaid lost them in a fair fight. It didn't take Slocum too much cogitating to decide the fight hadn't been fair. The Tennysons were backshooters and probably had never faced a man in a fair fight until Kincaid got around to gunning them down.

"Feel better?" Slocum asked.

"Not really," Kincaid allowed. He stared at the body strung over the second horse. He went over and spent several minutes picking at the knots with his bony fingers. Slocum went to help him. Two quick drags of his hunting knife sent Mark Tennyson slithering to the ground in a boneless pile. Putrefaction had set in and the corpse was drawing flies to beat the band.

Kincaid didn't offer any thanks. He rolled Tennyson's body over and looked down at it, as if seeing his victim for the first time. Then he spat.

"You wanting to bury these two?" asked Slocum. "We can put graves over there and—"

"No graves," Kincaid said coldly. "They don't deserve buryin'. No rites, no words, nothing."

Slocum studied the sheriff carefully. Those eyes drew him into a spiral that never seemed to end. Slocum pulled free and wondered why he was going along with the lawman. He was thin, pale and nothing more than skin and bones. A stiff breeze would knock over Abe Kincaid. And if Slocum argued over burying the Tennysons, what could the lawman really do?

He was fast, but so was Slocum. And Slocum now carried a full load in his Colt Navy.

"Is this worth getting into a fight over?" Slocum asked quietly. "I don't cotton to letting the buzzards and coyotes have any man, even sidewinders like these."

"No buryin'." Kincaid turned and widened his stance, ready to draw.

"It's worth shooting it out with me?" Slocum wondered what outrage the Tennyson gang had committed to cause such emotions to fester inside Kincaid.

"Reckon so." Kincaid stood like a statue, his eyes deader than either of the outlaws'.

"Tell me what went on. I can use a break." Slocum wasn't going to call out any sheriff, much less a gunman as fast and accurate as Kincaid. He might be just a touch faster, but Slocum wasn't willing to bet his life on it.

"I was sheriff in Buzzard Flats," Kincaid started, his voice level and colder than any Wyoming winter. "The whole Tennyson clan rode in just at sundown, drunk with power and thinking they owned the place because it was a small town. They shot up a few buildings, nothing serious, but annoying. I warned them, but the Tennysons didn't much listen. They kept hurrahing the town and shot up the saloon."

"Who'd they kill?" Slocum asked, beginning to understand the depth of Kincaid's feelings.

"Three patrons and a whore in the Wild Hare Saloon, including the owner. Old Gus was a good friend of mine. Couldn't let them get by with that. There'd never be any peace, if I had."

Slocum heard more in Kincaid's words than the man said. Simple murder was bad, but something had built this into a blood feud.

"Me and a couple deputies went after them. I lost the boys and their cousin Ethan, but I got their pa. John Tennyson put up a fight and wouldn't surrender."

"So you killed him." Slocum had heard of John "Two-bit" Tennyson but had never run across him. Now he understood why. He had been killed before his boys had taken up rustling.

"I shot him where he stood. Even if it hadn't been a fair fight, I would have blown him away. Standing trial would have been a waste of money. My only regret was not getting his filthy offspring at the same time."

"They came back for you?"

"Them? No, they didn't come back to face me like men. They began sniping at anyone in Buzzard Flats. Killed women and children as quick as they did armed men. Shot most of them in the back and then laughed about it. People started leaving, and I admit I was sore tempted to join them. But I didn't. I wanted them brought to justice for killing my town the way they did."

"Who else did they kill?" Slocum asked. He expected some reaction from Kincaid but didn't get it. The sheriff kept talking, as if reading down a list of supplies he needed for a hunting trip.

"My wife Lydia Anne got bushwhacked driving her buggy down yonder canyon." Kincaid made a vague gesture that seemed to encompass the entire valley and the red-walled canyon leading from it. "They never gave her a chance."

Kincaid turned and looked past Slocum, toward the canyon. "Ethan Crain's out there. I want him, too. He's younger than the others, but he is one of the family. For all I know, he might have had a hand in killing Lydia Anne."

"The town must have emptied pretty quick after your wife's murder," Slocum said.

"Buzzard Flats was never the same. Some just upped and left everything they had, running for another town. Others tried to pack their belongings and leave all orderly. Didn't matter which way they tried to leave. The Tennysons gunned them down."

Kincaid started walking for the grove. In the distance Slocum heard a horse snorting and pawing at the ground. Kincaid's mount was as anxious to capture Ethan Crain as its rider.

Slocum wanted to know what had happened then but Kincaid was on his way to bring the last of the Tennyson clan to justice. How he had lost his wedding ring and badge would be stories best told later, around a campfire, after they had finished bringing Crain to justice.

"You wanting some help, Sheriff?" called Slocum. "I got a score to settle with them, too. They killed David Stoner, tortured his father Immanuel and scared the hell out of the womenfolk."

"Do what you must." Kincaid never turned as he vanished into the woods. A few minutes later, he came riding out, stiff as a ramrod in the saddle and paler than a bleached sheet. Slocum wondered if Kincaid was consumptive. No man could be so pale and gaunt without having some killing disease.

Slocum got his Appaloosa and mounted, only to rein back and watch as Kincaid changed his path slightly. He rode to the pair of bodies on the ground. He reached behind him and began sprinkling something over the corpses. Then Kincaid fumbled in his pocket and got out a tin box. Slocum kept his horse under control as Kincaid flipped a lit lucifer onto the Tennysons.

He had doused them with kerosene and then ignited it. The bodies burned with a greasy smoke that curled high into the still air. Above, circled vultures, cheated of their meals.

As Kincaid rode past, he said, "No buryin'. They don't even deserve getting burned like they did my town, but no buryin'— and no prayin' over their miserable cadavers."

"I'm not much for that sort of thing," Slocum said. He put his heels to his Appaloosa's flanks and caught up with the lawman. Kincaid rode with eyes forward, his full attention on the canyon ahead. He didn't listen when Slocum warned him of possible Cheyenne war parties, and he didn't pay any attention at all when Slocum asked how he intended finding Ethan Crain.

Slocum had seen strange methods of tracking but nothing like that used by Abe Kincaid. The man rode along, oblivious to anything around him in the world, then would stop and turn slowly, left to right. Like a good hound scenting its quarry, he would change his path slightly and head off in a new direction.

The few times Slocum chose to look for spoor on his own convinced him Kincaid knew what he was doing. Ethan Crain had passed by, galloping hard. Some of the hoofprints crossed rock; this didn't slow Kincaid's tracking. Across streams, up and down, back and forth, nothing confused him. Even when Crain doubled back, obliterating his trail with a dragged bush as he went, Kincaid wasn't thrown off the trail. Slocum was a scout and tracker without peer—or so he had thought before seeing Abe Kincaid at work.

Kincaid was faster with a six-shooter and more accurate, and the best damned tracker Slocum had ever come across. That included more than a few Indians.

"We're close," Kincaid said unexpectedly. "Not more than a mile in that direction." He pointed and urged his reluctant horse down a steep embankment.

Slocum followed, more cautious. His sixth sense was beginning to warn him of danger. At the base of the slope, Kincaid rode off at an angle. Slocum took a different course, finding two familiar ruts in the ground. He kept Kincaid in view as he stopped beside the overturned buggy on the canyon floor.

Slocum stared at the bleached bones of the horse and remembered the handkerchief he had found. The monogram had been: LAK.

Lydia Anne Kincaid.

By sheer luck he had stumbled across the scene of the murder where the Tennysons had killed Abe Kincaid's wife. Slocum stared at the overturned buggy, as if expecting some answer to all his problems to be revealed. All Slocum heard was the mournful wail of wind blowing down the canyon and the soft sighing of pines along the upper rim of the canyon. The day was turning cool and the sun had slipped halfway behind the tall rock canyon edge. The entire canyon would be plunged into night within the hour.

The entire area seemed deserted, but Slocum grew increasingly edgy. He couldn't figure what was wrong, but something was. He didn't think Ethan Crain would turn and make a stand. He had taken off like a scalded dog. When Jeb Tennyson had called out to his cousin to meet in the usual place, wherever that might be, it gave Crain a destination. There wasn't any call to turn and fight, unless the belly wound was hurting him worse than Slocum thought.

He glanced down at the buggy once more and shuddered, not knowing why. Then he trotted after Kincaid, wanting to catch up with the sheriff and talk to him some more about the goings on in Buzzard Flats.

"Sheriff!" Slocum called after Kincaid. "Wait up." Kincaid didn't slow his deliberate pace, nor did he turn. He was a man obsessed with finding Ethan Crain and nothing would deter him.

Slocum caught up, angry at the sheriff for not even looking in his direction. He wasn't a man used to being ignored when he wanted to talk.

"You said the Tennysons shot up Buzzard Flats and hurrahed it." Slocum didn't get an answer or even the slightest acknowledgement he had asked a question. "They kept coming back. They weren't strangers to these parts, were they?"

"They had a hideout somewhere up in the hills," Kincaid said in his level voice. "Never did find it, but then I wasn't much looking for it. I wanted them, not the place they went to lick their wounds."

"Jeb told his cousin to head there when they separated," Slocum said, thinking hard. "What if Crain is circling to go back to Buzzard Flats?"

"What if he is?"

"The womenfolk back there aren't expecting any visitors, not like Ethan Crain," Slocum said. "We ought to ride faster, get over more toward the far canyon wall, and then we can be sure he doesn't double back on us."

"He's not," was all the answer Slocum got. Kincaid kept riding, occasionally changing direction as if some voice spoke only to him telling where Crain went. In the gathering gloom Slocum wasn't able to check the trail as often. After another twenty minutes of following Kincaid's lead, he decided doing his own tracking was a waste of effort. Even if Kincaid got off the trail, he knew the country better than anyone else.

If Kincaid lost Ethan Crain, he'd know where to start looking for him again.

"How long ago was the murder?" Slocum asked suddenly. Too many questions went unanswered for him. The blood on the buggy had been fresh, yet the horse was years dead. "Your wife. How long ago did the Tennysons kill her?"

"Well nigh five years," Kincaid answered. Slocum thought he detected a hint of emotion choking the sheriff's words, but he couldn't be sure. The wind was kicking up and turning the canyon floor colder than a knot on the North Pole. And they rode faster than he liked in the gathering gloom.

"Where have you been since then?" Slocum had danced around asking the obvious question too long. Either Kincaid answered or he didn't. Either way, Slocum's concern would be in the open. Kincaid have saved him, but that had been incidental. To kill Jeb Tennyson the man would have fought through a den of grizzly bears and spit in the face of a mountain lion.

Slocum pulled back on his reins and let Kincaid ride ahead, the sensation of impending danger almost too much to stand. Slocum cocked his head to one side and listened hard against the wind whipping out of the canyon mouth. Nothing unusual came to his ears. And no strange scent carried on the wind. Only feathers.

Slocum frowned when he saw a half dozen feathers blowing along the ground. They might have been turkey feathers.

"Kincaid, wait! We're riding into a trap!" Slocum shouted. But it was too late. The sheriff neared the edge of a small wooded area around a spring. From the deep shadows came a dozen Cheyenne braves, arrows nocked and ready to fly.

16

"Kincaid, look out! Cheyennes!" Slocum whipped out his six-shooter, wishing he had his rifle with him. He fired the Colt wildly, knowing he'd never hit anything at this range. All he wanted to do was spook the Indians and force them back into the forest. With a few seconds safe from their arrows, Slocum knew he and Kincaid could wheel around and get the hell out of the ambush.

But somehow, Kincaid didn't hear the warning or see the ambush. He kept riding, oblivious to even Slocum's shots. Slocum put his heels into the Appaloosa's sides and galloped forward, bending low by the horse's neck. He couldn't aim accurately on a running horse but he tried. Each shot he fired came as close to finding a target as he could have hoped. One Cheyenne brave even danced back, slapping at his hip. A bullet had come close enough to graze him.

Then came the rain of arrows Slocum had feared. The Cheyennes arched the arrows high, and they came down in a deadly blanket that no one could escape. Two arrows embedded in Slocum's saddle, and one drove past his shoulder, cutting a deep and bloody groove.

"Kincaid!" he shouted and still the lawman rode on, looking neither left nor right. He might have been in a trance, so complete was his concentration on tracking Ethan Crain.

Slocum's six-shooter came up empty. He kept racing toward the lawman, thinking to pull him from the saddle if necessary. As Slocum came even with Kincaid, the sheriff turned and stared at him with his infinitely deep, sad eyes.

"He's getting away," Kincaid said.

"Cheyenne, you damned fool. See?" Slocum yanked an arrow from his saddle and held it up for the lawman. He shook it hard and threw it from him. A new flight of arrows came at them. "We have to turn around, get back to high ground."

"Crain," muttered Kincaid. "He will get away if we do that. We cannot stop. *I* can't."

"We're being attacked by Indians. They'll have our scalps if we don't get out of here quick." Slocum fumbled to reload, but the Cheyennes weren't going to let him do that. They rushed forward, whooping and hollering, waving knives and shooting their bows as they came. The only bright spot was that none of the braves carried a rifle. Slocum and Kincaid would have been shot from their saddles if the Indians had repeating rifles.

Slocum wasn't going to argue with Kincaid. He put on a burst of speed that carried him past the edge of the Indian line. Slocum kicked out as he rode past, his boot catching a brave under the chin and snapping his head back. Two more arrows came singing out of the darkness toward him. He should have considered what the feathers blowing on the wind earlier had meant.

Braves had lost eagle feathers as they moved through the thicket along the bottom of this ravine. The wind had sent them fluttering as a warning to the wary. And Slocum had hardly understood their meaning until it was almost too late to respond.

Slocum heard Kincaid's horse behind him. He kept up a breakneck pace, dodging low limbs and twisting through the increasingly dense stand of trees. Worrying that he might be riding into an even riskier site didn't keep him back. Only death waited for him if he stayed in the exposed draw.

"There," Slocum gasped, pointing ahead. "We can make a stand there."

A tumble of rocks provided a barricade to fight behind. Slocum got his saddlebags free and hit the ground running. His Appaloosa followed, picking its way into the rocks behind him. Slocum dropped behind a large boulder and worked to reload his Colt. He barely got six rounds loaded when the Cheyenne came at him again.

He fired with measured speed and deadly accuracy. The Indians were so close Slocum killed one and wounded two more. This turned the brunt of their attack—for a few minutes. They weren't stupid. They had to know they had him trapped. All they needed to do was keep up the pressure and fire constantly. Sooner or later an arrow would find its mark, and a brave would gain a six-shooter and a scalp to brag over.

"Kincaid!" Slocum shouted. "Where are you?" He needed the lawman's gun beside him if he hoped to keep the Indians at bay much longer. To his surprise, Kincaid hadn't taken refuge with him. The sheriff rode on along the draw, chin high as if scenting the air and oblivious to everything around him.

Slocum knew the man wasn't crazy, though proving it now was something Slocum wouldn't care to try. Kincaid's charmed life kept him from being skewered by any of a dozen arrows whistling through the air around him. Then the sheriff vanished, and Slocum knew he was alone in his fight.

He reloaded again, wishing he had the spare Colt Navy he had given Sarah. Two six-shooters would increase his chances of escaping with his hair still in place. As it was, he had to hold back a round or two after every onslaught to be sure he could stop the most aggressive of his attackers.

"Want to parlay?" Slocum shouted, hoping a war chief might decide to talk. All Slocum got for his trouble was another quick skirmish and a new wound on his upper left arm. He bled slowly from a couple dozen minor wounds. Falling down the hillside when he'd tried to ambush the Tennysons had taken its toll, but the wounds he received now were deeper, more serious, and they burned like liquid fire.

A slight scraping sound alerted Slocum that one brave had gotten behind him. He didn't try to use the Colt. He laid it half-loaded onto the rock in front of him and whirled about, drawing his hunting knife. Slocum lifted the tip just enough to drive it into the Indian's belly as he jumped from the rocks above. The Cheyenne brave slashed feebly with his own knife, but the back of the blade raked across Slocum's forehead—the unsharpened back edge. A deep bruise might spring up, but he wasn't blinded.

Or killed.

Slocum turned back and saw a dozen Cheyennes making for him at a dead run. He had four chambers loaded. He used all four bullets to stop the leading Indian. This caused the others to break off, to reconsider their frontal attack.

Slocum knew he would die where he stood without a bold counter. He reloaded two chambers and stood, bellowing loudly. He rushed the Cheyenne and momentarily routed them. Whistling, he got his Appaloosa down from the rocks and jumped into the saddle.

More arrows sought his back—and one lodged in his upper leg. Slocum broke off the fletched end and kept riding. His only chance lay in outdistancing the war party. And the way he had ridden so foolishly into the ambush, Slocum wasn't looking to luck any longer.

He jerked when two arrows embedded in his boot, one in the heel and the other in the thick leather a few inches higher up. The arrowhead scraped against his leg, more irritating than dangerous. Slocum wished he had his six-shooter loaded again. The feeling of triumph when he had turned and attacked the Indians was gratifying. If he was going to die, he'd rather have an arrow in the forehead than one in the back.

"Slocum, here," came Kincaid's cold voice. "I found the trail again. Crain must have gotten turned around."

"The Cheyennes," grated out Slocum, feeling blood running down his leg and filling his right boot. "They're hot on my ass!"

Abe Kincaid looked from Slocum to the trail behind, as if noticing the Cheyenne war party for the first time. He drew his gun and began shooting. Slocum wasn't sure he hit anything, but the war whoops died down. Turning and glancing over his shoulder, Slocum saw the Cheyenne breaking off their assault. They huddled together like frightened children, pointing at Kincaid and then moving back into the woods.

"I don't know what's with them," Slocum said, wincing as hot pain turned his entire body into a branding iron. "They had me once before, when I was tracking the sodbusters. They drew back and wouldn't go toward Buzzard Flats."

Kincaid said nothing. He carefully reloaded and stood in his stirrups to get a better look, not at the Indians but at the ground where he had found Crain's trail.

"There. He was heading straight out the canyon, then he doubled back. Maybe he thinks he can throw me off the path that way."

"He ran afoul of the Indians and got away without them seeing him," Slocum said, stating the obvious. "Crain didn't have the ammo or will to fight a couple dozen braves." The world twisted around as shock set in. Slocum hung onto the reins for dear life.

"He's got an hour or more on us along the trail," Kincaid said in his monotone voice, not giving up on finding Crain for even a second. He walked his horse slowly back down the rocky draw, back toward the mouth of the canyon and the rocky red butte marking the entrance to the valley where Buzzard Flats lay so deserted and still. Now and again, Kincaid turned as if listening to some inner voice, and always he kept moving.

Slocum spent as much time looking over his shoulder as he did riding along. He knew better than to try to walk. Occasionally dizzy from the loss of blood, he vowed to keep moving. If Kincaid could track all night, so could he.

But when Slocum almost fell from his horse, Kincaid took notice of his condition.

"Those Indians did you up good. You need some patching before you can ride on." Kincaid pulled Slocum from the saddle, careful not to aggravate the wounds made by the Cheyenne arrows.

"We have to keep going," Slocum said. "They'll be after us." He felt a touch feverish but knew the Cheyennes never gave up. They were fierce fighters ever since Sweet Medicine had organized them into fighting bands over at Devils Tower. Slocum had heard tell of Dull Knife growing increasingly restive about the government's decision to put all red men on reservations in Indian Territory. And the war party was after him, and he had to keep running.

Slocum snapped back to cold reality when he felt Kincaid's hand on his forehead.

"You're running a mite of fever," the sheriff said quietly. "Nothing to worry over. I seen worse. We'll get Ethan Crain. Bet on it."

Slocum focused again on their mission. "What if he gets back to Buzzard Flats before we do? He'll have hostages once more. We can't let that happen." All Slocum could think of was Sarah and her mother. Immanuel Stoner must have died by now, him doing so poorly when Slocum had left. At least he had been surrounded by his people when he died.

If Crain and his cousins had killed once, they had killed dozens of times. Adding notches on his six-gun for two more women might seem like revenge for the Tennysons' cousin.

"Why didn't you stay with me back there? When the Cheyennes first attacked? You ran off and let me guard your rear." Slocum pushed himself to a sitting position. The dizziness had passed, and he was feeling thirsty, a good sign. And his belly grumbled from lack of food. Most of his cuts were shallow, and the few deep ones had caked over. He had been injured worse than this more times than he wanted to remember. What bothered him most was the arrow he had taken in the thigh. And the hunger. Slocum thought his stomach was grinding into his backbone he was so hungry.

"Stay? I was after Crain. Can't let anything come between me and him. There's so little time left. Got to keep tracking and find him." Kincaid turned his oddly disturbing gaze on Slocum and asked a strange question.

"What day is it? What day?"

Slocum struggled to remember. "I left the wagon train two-three days back," he said, sorting dates out in his mind. "We'd been on the trail for some time. That makes today March twentieth."

"March twentieth," Kincaid said, rolling the words over and over as if savoring them. "There's enough time."

"Time for what?" asked Slocum. He rubbed his thigh and got some circulation back into it. He worked his boot free and tended the scratch on his calf. The blood in the boot would have to be washed out later. Now didn't seem the time.

Kincaid didn't answer. Rather, he asked an even stranger question. "What's the year? You got to tell me. What year is it?"

"Same as it was last month and the month before," Slocum allowed. "Eighteen-seventy-two."

Kincaid almost smiled, the closest Slocum had seen the man come to showing any true emotion. He turned and stared into the dark, humming a tuneless song to himself.

"I'll be able to ride soon enough," Slocum said. He stood and tried his weight on his right leg. Both the calf and thigh hurt like a hill of red ants had taken up residence inside his skin, but moving didn't open the wounds and even loosened the muscles enough for Slocum to mount.

He pulled arrows free from the leather in the saddle and made sure none of the Cheyenne war arrows had penetrated to cut the Appaloosa's hide. Only then did Slocum call out to Kincaid, "Let's get to tracking. I don't want him holding the ladies hostage."

"He'll head straight back to Buzzard Flats," Kincaid said in an almost dreamy tone. "He doesn't have any choice. He *has* to go there so I can—" Kincaid bit off the rest of his sentence and spat, as if it tasted bitter on his tongue. The sheriff heaved to his feet and walked to his horse. For a moment, Slocum thought Kincaid wasn't going to make it.

The man had always appeared weak, gaunt, undernourished. Now he wobbled as he walked. It was as if their fight with the Tennysons had finally drained Kincaid of all vitality. His hands resting on the reins and pommel were frail, aged, and parchment-like. His face had a sunken appearance reminding Slocum of corpses he had seen.

But Kincaid's eyes blazed with an inner force that was undeniable. His body might be weak but the spirit was strong, as strong as any Slocum had ever encountered.

"That way's Buzzard Flats," Kincaid said, leading the way. The sheriff had no trouble picking up the faint spoor left by the fleeing outlaw, and Slocum never questioned how Kincaid so unerringly kept to the trail.

Slocum let his Appaloosa pick the way through the darkness. The sliver of moon was almost gone and gave no illumination for the ride. He dozed as he rode, still weak from blood loss and gnawing hunger. After they had finished Ethan Crain, Slocum promised himself a nice, thick steak and a bottle of whiskey.

And Sarah. He'd have Sarah with him. They would—what? Slocum came awake and wiped at sweat on his forehead. He had been dreaming of Sarah. What did she really mean to him, and what did he mean to her? She was rebelling from an overly strict father who would move rather than have his daughter fall in with a man of shaky reputation.

Frank, Slocum remembered. That had been the name Sarah told him. Her swain back in Missouri. Slocum realized Sarah might have taken up with him the way she did to rebel against her father and even to dull the memory of Frank. Slocum might never mean as much to Sarah as her first true love.

What kind of life could he offer any woman? There were wanted posters drifting around the West, some bearing a pretty fair likeness on them. Judge killers had to keep moving before someone recognized them. And Slocum's life hadn't been lily-white. A train or two had been robbed, and stagecoaches and even a bank had fallen when he couldn't get decent work. When he did find an honest job, such as scouting for Carter's wagon train, it didn't pay a whole lot.

He had more in his pocket from robbing a dead man than Carter was likely to pay him before they reached Oregon. Still, Slocum had been a fair farmer at one time, and his skills in the wilderness could keep a family in game all year round.

"You look half dead. Don't go dyin' on me until we find Crain," said Kincaid.

"I can make it," Slocum said, knowing he was lying. He was almost ready to keel over. His straying thoughts about Sarah and settling down and what it might mean proved that. He belonged under a blanket of stars, moving with the herds, keeping one county ahead of the law. Freedom. That meant the most of Slocum.

"The hell you can. I need you tomorrow, Slocum. We got time. It's only the twentieth. We can be in Buzzard Flats before noon."

"Why's that so important?"

Slocum didn't get an answer because he might have passed out. When he came to, he was flat on his back and staring up into the sky. He tried counting stars to prove to himself he could ride on, but when they blurred and danced about in wild circles, he knew he had to rest.

"You go on to sleep. I'll keep watch," Kincaid said, hunkered down by a small fire. "We'll make it to Buzzard Flats in plenty of time."

Slocum saw the sheriff sit on his haunches and gaze into the fire, as if he could see the future in the crackling embers and darting, ever-shifting flames. Slocum knew Kincaid wouldn't sleep. He was too keyed up thinking about getting Ethan Crain.

As he drifted off to sleep, Slocum heard distant gunfire, horses neighing in pain, and the screams of tortured men and women.

17

Slocum awoke just before sunrise, his hand resting on his six-shooter. The campfire had died down but Kincaid still sat, staring into the cold pit as if he hadn't moved a muscle all night long. As Slocum stirred, the sheriff turned toward him.

"Time to get moving," Kincaid said. "It's time."

"It's past time," Slocum said, struggling to sit up. His belly complained, but the water from a canteen Kincaid handed him went a ways toward quelling the noise. He had been hungry before and for less good reason. Taking time now to hunt a rabbit and fix it or even scrounge around for some berries took away from finding Ethan Crain. Slocum regretted having to sleep away most of the night, but his strength had returned.

"What are you planning?" he asked Kincaid. The man accepted the canteen back from Slocum but didn't drink. Kincaid corked it and slung the canteen over his shoulder, as if thinking hard on the question.

"We find Crain. I kill him. It's that simple."

"You're not looking to arrest him?" Slocum got to his feet and stretched. He drew his Colt a couple times, making sure it rode easy on his hip and was available when he needed it.

"No need. Not a court in this country would do anything but stretch his neck. Are you going to talk or ride?" Kincaid finished saddling his horse and waited for Slocum to get his Appaloosa ready. Slocum swung into the saddle a few minutes after Kincaid.

"Why didn't you go on and leave me last night? You're all het up to get Crain. I'm a burden." Slocum watched the lawman carefully for any sign of emotion. None came to the hatchet-thin face.

"It'll take two of us to flush him out. Don't ask how I know. I just do," said Kincaid. "He's back in Buzzard Flats."

"That town draws men like flies to shit," Slocum said. "Why doesn't Crain just keep on riding if he thinks you will track him back there?"

"Can't. Can't do that any more than I can—" Kincaid snapped his mouth shut and rode stolidly, eyes ahead.

The silence gave Slocum time to think, too, and he didn't like the ideas boiling to the top. Ethan Crain returning to Buzzard Flats meant the Stoner women were in trouble again. Slocum hadn't given his spare six-shooter to Sarah thinking she would really be able to use it. It had been nothing more than a crutch for her confidence, something to make her think she could cope on her own. Against a killer like Crain, she and her ma were babes-in-the-woods.

But why did Crain return when he could as easily keep on riding? Sheer meanness was an excuse for a lot of the outlaw's behavior but survival meant something, too. Crain knew Kincaid—or Slocum—would come after him. Slocum didn't take him to be a brave enough man to make a stand. He'd run like a scalded dog, especially if he had seen the band of Cheyenne and been spooked by them.

Slocum licked his lips as he considered the way he had been behaving. Something pulled him back into Buzzard Flats again and again. Sarah had acted strangely out of character for her, and then there was Abe Kincaid. Beyond that, why didn't the Cheyenne war party finish him off when they had the chance? Twice braves had come close to wearing his scalp on a belt and twice they had backed off.

GHOST TOWN 159

When Kincaid had finally noticed the Indians and started firing, they had turned tail and run. It had been twenty of them against two. The odds favored the Cheyennes.

"We can get him. You go in one end of town and flush him toward me. He's not going to run once I got him in my sights." Kincaid touched the worn butt of the six-shooter hanging at his hip.

Slocum nodded, wondering what Kincaid really planned. The last time, when he had gunned down Mark Tennyson, he had simply vanished. Slocum wanted to be sure that wouldn't happen this time but didn't know exactly how to go about asking. By the time he had everything straight in his head, Kincaid was gone.

Slocum looked around, twisting in all directions. Kincaid might have been mist in the morning sun for all the noise he'd made leaving. Slocum rubbed his forehead, worrying that he might not be up to facing Ethan Crain. He was a tracker, a scout and damned good at it, yet Kincaid had simply . . . vanished.

Nearing the outskirts of Buzzard Flats, Slocum slowed and grew cautious. The cries the night before had been phantoms in his feverish brain, but the silence he met now was more worrisome than all the gunfire in the world.

Dropping to the ground, Slocum drew his Colt Navy and walked into the town on foot. He wanted to see Sarah running up to him, arms ready to circle his neck. He'd even be satisfied with Lottie Stoner's sour look or Immanuel Stoner's gruff denial that anything was wrong. Slocum saw neither of the women, but he did spy the man.

Immanuel Stoner lay under the damaged wagon, moaning in pain. This startled Slocum. He had reckoned the man would be dead by now. Stoner was tougher than he had any right to be.

Slocum walked a few more yards, then began wiggling on his belly like a snake to get closer to the man. Stoner rested in the shade of the wagon, but there wasn't any sign of the two women. Slocum knew they both wouldn't leave unless there was a powerful good reason.

"Where are they, Stoner?" Slocum whispered. "Has Crain got them?"

"Hurt them. He'll hurt them," Stoner gasped out. His eyelids flickered open. He reached out and gripped Slocum's sleeve with weak fingers. "Don't let him have them, Slocum. Get him. Get him and stop him!"

"Where are they?"

Slocum had pushed the man beyond his limits. Stoner sank weakly to the ground, shaking as if he had the ague. The man hadn't told Slocum any more than he had already guessed. Ethan Crain had Sarah and Lottie Stoner—but where?

"The Wild Hare Saloon," Slocum said to himself. The building was intact. That would be the spot where Crain would be most secure.

Slocum rolled from under the wagon and took a roundabout route getting to the saloon. He saw that his guess had been good. A horse, lathered from a hard ride, was tethered outside the saloon. And from inside came loud, off-key music as someone played the battered piano. It wouldn't be Crain doing the playing. That meant at least one of the women was at the keyboard.

A broken-out window gave Slocum a look inside. He saw Lottie Stoner at the piano, struggling to get a tune out of the disintegrating keyboard. Behind her stood Ethan Crain, a six-gun in his holster and a rifle laying in the crook of his arm. He had more firepower, but Slocum knew what to do. Waiting for Abe Kincaid was out of the question.

Slocum leveled his Colt Navy for the killing shot. He hastily ducked back when Crain turned, the rifle muzzle pressed against Lottie Stoner's head.

"You keep on playin', you hear? I want it to be lively. Like them can-can songs they play." Crain laughed and shouted, "You got that dress on yet?"

Slocum saw Sarah coming down the rickety stairs, wearing the same dress she had when they had made love in the upstairs cribs. This time her expression wasn't as happy. She was pale and her hands shook as she made her way down to the saloon floor.

GHOST TOWN 161

"Get on up there on the bar and start dancin'. I want to see them legs of yours. Kick up your knees, now, just like them dance-hall fillies do. Years back there was a filly what looked the world like you. Yes, sir, you surely do remind me of poor ole Samantha." Crain laughed harshly and added, "It was a damned shame when I had to kill her."

Slocum paused, remembering what Kincaid had said about a whore being gunned down by the Tennyson gang. Somehow, Crain was reliving those days, and Sarah had became a part of the playacting.

Slocum tried to get a good shot at Crain again. Once more the way the man shoved his rifle against Lottie Stoner's head kept Slocum from firing. If he hit Crain and didn't kill him outright, the outlaw would blow off Mrs. Stoner's head. And even if Slocum got him with one shot, muscles convulsed and he still might end an innocent's life. Slocum had to try something more.

He picked up a rock and heaved it hard across the street. It clattered against a wall and sent echoes from one end of Buzzard Flats to the other. Ethan Crain swung around and rushed to the front door to see what was happening. This was all the opening Slocum needed.

He fired at the outlaw's back and cursed when he only winged Crain. He fired again, driving the last of the Tennyson gang into the street.

"Get down!" Slocum shouted to the women. "Take cover."

He tumbled into the saloon, ready to keep firing if Ethan Crain poked his head back inside. He made his way to Sarah, who hugged him and said, "John, I knew you'd get back to save us."

She kissed him, but Slocum pushed her away. He didn't think he had wounded Crain too bad, not from the way the man scuttled off like a crab.

"Get away from the windows," he called to Lottie Stoner, who just sat and stared at the piano's keyboard, as if she was frozen to the spot. She looked up at him with dull gray eyes.

"I have to play," she said.

"Sarah, get your ma behind the bar," Slocum ordered. "If I don't stop Crain now, that son of a bitch is going to get away again." He reloaded the rounds he had fired, wanting a full cylinder when he caught up with Ethan Crain.

"You're not going to leave us?" Sarah bit her lower lip and looked aggrieved at this treatment. "He . . . he might come back and—"

"Damned right he will, unless I put enough lead in him to stop him once and for all." Slocum pushed her away and went to the door. Sarah said something, but Slocum was already stalking Ethan Crain. He wanted the outlaw so bad he could taste it.

Tracking in the town was something of a problem. Slocum cocked his head to one side and listened hard, trying to make out the sound of boots against wood. Crain either had gone to ground or was staying in the dusty streets. For more than fifteen minutes Slocum hunted for Crain, not finding hide nor hair of the outlaw. Instead of hunting, Slocum decided it was time to start thinking. When the answer came to him, he cursed himself for being such a fool.

He ran pell-mell back to Immanuel Stoner. Slocum skidded to a halt when he saw what Crain had done.

"I thought it was you, cowboy. Now what are you going to do?" Crain held a lucifer near a black miner's fuse. Slocum knew blasting and saw there was less than a foot cut—less than one minute of burn.

"You're a dead man, Crain. I swear. Let him go. You damned near killed him, anyway."

"Almost killed him," Crain corrected. He lit the fuse. It ran down the length of black fuse and branched out to four other fuses, each ending in a stick of dynamite. "It's a good thing we found a box of this stuff in the storehouse. I figured I might need some of this here dynamite. You choose what you want to do."

Crain ducked behind the wagon and then ran like hell. Slocum got to the wagon and saw he wouldn't have time to go after Crain and save Immanuel Stoner. He didn't even have time to snuff out the fuses running all over like some wild tangle of string left behind by a playful kitten. Crain hadn't spent much time laying the fuse, but it was effective.

Slocum pulled Stoner from under the wagon by the heels and hoisted him over his shoulder. He started walking—and was helped along the way when a stick of dynamite went off. The force of the explosion sent Slocum stumbling hard. He kept his feet only to be blown to the ground by a second stick of exploding dynamite. Slocum lay dazed, staring at the blue sky above Buzzard Flats and wondering if this was what it felt like to be dead.

From a distance he heard Sarah's voice. An angel? He struggled to sit up, but the world swung in wide circles around him.

"You saved him, you did! What blew up, John? You saved him. We saw it!"

"Crain," Slocum said, shaking himself like a wet dog. That helped get his senses back. He glanced down and saw Immanuel Stoner was still alive. That man would live to be a hundred. He was just too cussed to ever die.

"Don't, John. Let him go. We can get out of town. Father's—" Slocum cut the young woman off.

"I want Crain." He got to his feet and stumbled along, growing stronger with every step. Over his shoulder he yelled, "Get your pa in the other wagon. Clear out."

"But, John, you—"

"Now!" Slocum bellowed. He ran after Crain, rounding the livery stable just in time to see the tableau. Crain and Abe Kincaid stood less than fifteen feet apart. Crain's hand shook so hard Slocum thought it might break off.

"Draw," was all Kincaid said.

It was a fair fight. Ethan Crain went for his gun, but Kincaid's draw was almost invisible it was so fast. The sheriff fired, and the bullet caught Crain smack in the center of his face. The outlaw dropped like a marionette with its strings cut. Never had Slocum seen any man draw faster or shoot more accurately than Abe Kincaid.

"You beat me to him," Slocum said, coming up beside the lawman. "You got all three of them."

"It's March twenty first," Kincaid said, turning and walking off. "Time's up."

"Don't go off like this," Slocum called. He thought Crain was dead but checked anyway. The outlaw had tortured his last victim. Kincaid's bullet had left a bloody mess where the back of Crain's head had been, though the entry point between his eyes was hardly more than a small red dot.

Slocum turned and looked for Kincaid. The sheriff was gone. And hunt as he might, Slocum couldn't find any trace of the lawman in Buzzard Flats.

Walking quickly, Slocum got back to the Stoner women. They had piled Immanuel Stoner into the rear of the good wagon and were trying to get the oxen to pulling. As Slocum walked by, he slapped one on the rump and got the team pulling hard. It was a waste to leave two good oxen behind, not to mention the other wagon and most of its contents, but Slocum wasn't in any mood to care.

He wanted to leave Buzzard Flats and nothing was going to stop him now.

"Get onto the road back to the canyon," Slocum said, knowing they might encounter the Cheyenne again. But somehow he thought the Indians had already hightailed it for parts unknown. They had faced Abe Kincaid's gun and wouldn't be inclined to stay any longer than necessary. "I'll catch up."

"Yes, John," Sarah said. Lottie Stoner sat in the rear of the wagon, beside her husband. He stirred restlessly, the only sign of life left to him.

Slocum hurried to his Appaloosa and mounted. He watched as Sarah got the wagon back onto the faint road leading from Buzzard Flats. Slocum made one last search of the town for any trace of Abe Kincaid and found nothing.

"To hell with you all," he said and spat toward the center of town. Slocum rode fast to catch up with Sarah's wagon, but he reined to a halt when he saw the cemetery and the fresh tracks by it.

A solitary rider had entered recently. Slocum looked around for Kincaid but didn't see the sheriff. On impulse,

Slocum dismounted and walked into the cemetery, following the tracks—to a pair of graves set back at the rear.

"Lydia Anne Kincaid," Slocum read slowly from the tombstone. And beside it was a second grave.

Abraham Kincaid. October 12, 1849—March 21, 1877.

"You came back and got them, five years to the day after they put you six feet under," Slocum said. He didn't much understand why Kincaid had shown himself the way he had, or why he and the Stoners had been caught up in the deadly retribution, but Slocum didn't have anyone to question about it. He had played out the role fate had ordained for him, and that was good enough explanation. Slocum tipped his hat in salute to a man who knew what he wanted and got it, even from beyond the grave. Slocum got back on his Appaloosa and rode away, not looking back.

He had to catch up with Sarah and her mother and get them back to the wagon train. That would take a heap of doing. Maybe Abe Kincaid would be there along the way with his fast gun to help out. But Slocum wasn't counting on it, not after seeing the gravestones.

After rejoining the wagon train, John Slocum just didn't know what he would do. And as he thought on it, that wasn't so bad. Life shouldn't be any more predictable than death.

*Turn the page for an exciting preview
of the newest Western novel
by the acclaimed author of* Texas Legends

GENE SHELTON

They were unlikely partners: a Yankee gentleman and a Rebel hellraiser. They met in a barroom brawl, and the only thing they had in common was the law on their tails. Flat broke, and on the run, they had nothing to lose by trying something crazy—like going into business together ...

TEXAS HORSETRADING CO.

*A rousing epic of the Wild West
available now from Diamond Books!*

The last thing Brubs McCallan remembered was a beer bottle headed straight for the bridge of his nose.

Now he came awake in a near panic, a cold, numbing fear that he had gone blind. Beyond the stabbing pain in his head he could make out only jerky, hazy shapes.

Brubs sighed with relief as he realized he was only in jail.

The shapes were hazy and indistinct partly because only a thin, weak light filtered into the cell from the low flame of a guttering oil lamp on a shelf outside the bars. And the shapes were fuzzy partly because his left eye was swollen almost shut.

Brubs leaned back against the thin blankets on the hard wooden cot and groaned. The movement sent the sledgehammer in his head to pounding a fresh set of spikes through his temples.

"Good morning."

Brubs started at the sound of the voice. He tried to focus his good eye on the dim form on the cot across the room. He could tell that the man was tall. His boots stuck out past the end of the cot. He had an arm hooked behind his head for a pillow, his hat pulled down over his eyes. "Mornin' yourself,"

Brubs mumbled over a swollen lower lip. "Question is, which mornin' is it, anyway?"

"Sunday, I believe. How do you feel?"

"Like I had a boot hung up in the stirrup and got drug over half of Texas." Brubs lifted a hand to his puffy face and heard the scratch of his palm against stubble. "And like somebody swabbed the outhouse with my tongue. Other than that, passin' fair."

"Glad to hear that. I was afraid that beer bottle might have caused some permanent damage."

Brubs swung his feet over the edge of the cot, sat up, and immediately regretted it. The hammer slammed harder against the spikes in his brain. He squinted at the tall man on the bunk across the way. "I remember you," he said after a moment. "How come you whopped me with that beer bottle?"

"I couldn't find an ax handle and you were getting the upper hand on me at the time," the man said.

Brubs wiggled his nose between a thumb and forefinger. "At least you didn't bust my beak again," he said. "That would have plumb made me mad. I done broke it twice the last year and a half. What was we fightin' about?"

The tall man swung his feet over the side of the cot and sat, rubbing a hand across the back of his neck. "You don't remember? After all, you started it."

"Oh. Yeah, I reckon it's comin' back now. But that cowboy was cheatin'. Seen him palm a card on his deal." Brubs snorted in disgust. "Wasn't even good at cheatin'."

"How do you know that?"

"If he'd been any good I wouldn't of caught him. I can't play poker worth a flip. Who pulled him off me?"

"I did."

"What'd you do that for? I had him right where I wanted him. I was hittin' him square in the fist with my face ever' time he swung. Another minute or two, I'd of had him wore plumb down."

"I didn't want to interfere, but I saw him reach for a knife. That didn't seem fair in a fistfight."

Brubs sighed. "You're dead right about that. That when I belted you?"

"The first time."

Brubs heaved himself unsteadily to his feet. It wasn't easy. Brubs packed a hundred and sixty pounds of mostly muscle on a stubby five-foot-seven frame, and it seemed to him that every one of those muscles was bruised, stretched, or sore. Standing up didn't help his head much, either.

The man on the other bunk raised a hand. "If you don't mind, I'd just as soon not start it again. I don't have a beer bottle with me at the moment."

"Aw, hell," Brubs said, "I wasn't gonna start nothin'. Just wanted to say I'm obliged you didn't let that cowboy stick a knife in my gizzard." He strode stiffly to the side of the bunk and offered a hand. "Brubs McCallan."

The man on the cot stood. He was a head taller than Brubs, lean and wiry, built along the lines of a mountain cat where Brubs tended toward the badger clan. The lanky man took Brubs's hand. His grip was firm and dry. "Dave Willoughby. Nice to make your acquaintance under more civilized conditions."

"Wouldn't call the San Antonio jail civilized," Brubs said with a grin. The smile started his split lower lip to leaking blood again. He released Willoughby's hand. "We tear the place up pretty good?"

"My last recollection is that we had made an impressive start to that end," Willoughby said. "Shortly thereafter, somebody blew the lantern out on me, too."

Both men turned as a door creaked open and bootsteps sounded. The oil lamp outside the cell flared higher as a stocky man twisted the brass key of the wick feeder with a thick hand. The light spilled over a weathered face crowned by an unruly thatch of gray hair. "What's all the yammering about? Gettin' so a man can't sleep around here anymore."

The stocky man stood with the lamp held at shoulder height. A ring of keys clinked as he hobbled to the cell. His left knee was stiff. He had to swing the leg in a half circle when he walked. The lamplight glittered from a badge on his vest and the brass back strap of a big revolver holstered high on his right hip.

"You the sheriff?" Brubs asked.

"Night deputy. Sheriff don't come on duty for another couple hours. Name's Charlie Purvis. If you boys are gonna be the guests of Bexar County for a while, you better learn to keep it quiet when I'm on duty."

"We will certainly keep that in mind, Deputy Purvis," Dave Willoughby said. "We apologize for having disturbed you. We will be more reserved in the future."

Brubs glared through his one open eye at the deputy. "What do you mean, guests of the county?"

"In case you boys ain't heard," the deputy said, "that brawl you started over at the Longhorn just about wrecked the place. I don't figure you two've got enough to pay the fines and damages."

Dave sighed audibly. "How much might that be, Deputy?"

"Twenty-dollar fine apiece for startin' the fight and disturbin' the peace. Thirty-one dollars each for damages. Plus a dime for the beer bottle you busted over your friend's head."

"What?" Brubs's voice was a startled croak. "You gonna charge this man a dime for whoppin' me with a beer bottle?"

The deputy shrugged. "Good glass bottles are hard to find out here. Owner of the Longhorn says they're worth a dime apiece."

Brubs snorted in disgust. "Damnedest thing I ever heard." He glanced up at Willoughby. "Good thing you didn't hit me with the back bar mirror. God knows what that would of cost. You got any money, Dave?"

Willoughby rummaged in a pocket and poked a finger among a handful of coins. "Thirty-one cents."

Brubs sighed in relief. "Good. There for a minute I was afraid we was plumb broke." He fumbled in his own pocket. "I got seventeen cents. Had four dollars when I set in on that poker game."

"Looks like you boys got troubles," Purvis said, shaking his shaggy head. "Can't let you out till the fines and damages are paid."

"How we gonna pay if we're in jail?"

Purvis shrugged. "Should have thought about that before you decided to wreck the Longhorn. Guess you'll just have to work it out on the county farm."

"Farm!" Brubs sniffed in wounded indignation and held out his hands. "These look like farmer's hands?"

The deputy squinted. "Nope. Don't show no sign of work if you don't count the skinned knuckles." Purvis grinned. "They'll toughen up quick on a hoe handle. We got forty acres in corn and cotton, and ten weeds for every crop plant. Pay's four bits a day." He scratched his jaw with a thick finger. "Let's see, now—fifty cents a day, you owe fifty-one dollars. . . . Works out to a hundred and two days. Each."

Dave Willoughby sighed. "Looks like it's going to be a long summer."

Purvis plucked a watch from his vest pocket, flipped the case open, and grunted. "Near onto sunup. You boys wrecked my nap. Might as well put some coffee on." He snapped the watch shut. "I reckon the county can spare a couple cups if you two rowdies want some."

Brubs scrubbed a hand over the back of his neck. "I'll shoot anybody you want for a cup of coffee. Got anything for hangovers? I got a size twelve headache in a size seven head."

The deputy chuckled. "Sympathy's all I got to offer. Know how you feel. I been there, back in my younger days. Busted up a saloon or two myself. You boys sit tight. I'll be back in a few minutes with the coffee."

Brubs trudged back to the cot and sat, elbows propped against his knees. He became aware of a gray light spreading through the cell and glanced at the wall above Dave's bunk. A small, barred rectangle high above the floor brightened with the approaching dawn. "Well, Dave," Brubs said after a moment, "you sure got us in a mess this time."

Willoughby turned to face Brubs, a quizzical expression on his face. "*I* got us in a mess? I was under the impression that you started the fight and I was the innocent bystander."

Brubs shrugged as best he could without moving his throbbing head. "Don't matter. Question now is, how do we break out of here?"

Willoughby raised a hand, palm out. "Wait a minute—you can't be serious! Breaking out of jail is a felony offense. We would be wanted criminals, possibly with a price on our heads. If you're thinking of escape, even if it was possible, count me out."

Brubs prodded his puffy eyebrow with a finger. The swelling seemed to be going down some. "I ain't working for the county, Dave. 'Specially not on some damn farm." He squinted at his free hand. "These hands don't fit no hoe handle. That's how come I left home in the first place."

Willoughby strode to his own bunk and stretched out on his back. "Where's home?"

"Nacogdoches, I reckon. Never had a real home to call it such." He raised his undamaged eyebrow at Willoughby. "You sure talk funny. Since we're tradin' life stories here, where you from?"

"Cincinnati."

"That on the Sabine or the Red River?"

"Neither. It's on the Ohio."

Brubs moaned. "Oh, Christ. I'm sittin' here tryin' my best to die from day-old whiskey, I got my butt whupped in a saloon fight, I owe money I ain't got, I been threatened with choppin' cotton, and now it turns out I'm sharin' a cell with a Yankee. If I hadn't had such a damn good time last night, I'd be plumb disgusted."

A faint smile flitted over Willoughby's face. "I suppose it was a rather interesting diversion, at that." He winced and probed the inside of his cheek with his tongue. "I think you chipped one of my teeth. For a little man, you swing a mean punch."

The creak of the door between cell block and outer office brought both men to their feet. Brubs could smell the coffee before the deputy came into view, carrying two tin cups on a flat wooden slab. Purvis crouched stiffly and slid the cups through the grub slot of the cell.

Brubs grabbed a cup, scorched his fingers on the hot tin, sipped at the scalding liquid, and sighed, contented. "Mother's milk for a hung over child," he said. "If I was a preacher I'd bless your soul, Charlie Purvis."

Purvis straightened slowly, the creak of his joints clearly audible. "You boys'll get some half-raw bacon and burnt biscuits when the sheriff gets here. Need anything else meantime?"

"I don't reckon you could see your way clear to leave the key in the lock?" Brubs asked hopefully.

Purvis shook his head. "Couldn't do that." He pointed toward a dark smear on the adobe wall near the door of the office. "Just in case you boys got some ideas perkin' along with the headaches, study on that spot over there. That's what's left of the last man tried to bust out of my jail." He clucked his tongue. "Sure did hate to cut down on him with that smoothbore. Double load of buckshot splattered guts all over the place. Made a downright awful mess. Why, pieces of that fellow were—"

"I think we understand your message, Deputy," Willoughby interrupted with a wince. "If you don't mind, spare us the gory details."

The deputy shrugged. "Well, I'll leave you boys to your chicken pluckin'. Sure don't envy you none. It gets hotter than the devil's kitchen out in those fields in summer."

Brubs moaned aloud at the comment.

"Is there somebody who could help us?" Willoughby asked. "A bondsman, perhaps, or someone who would loan us the money to get out of here?"

Charlie Purvis frowned. "Might be one man. I'm not sure you'd like the deal, though."

"Charlie," Brubs said, pleading, "I'd make a deal with Old Scratch himself to keep my hands off a damn hoe handle."

The deputy shrugged. "Same difference, maybe. But I'll talk to him." Purvis turned and limped away. The door creaked shut behind him.

Brubs stopped pacing the narrow cell and glanced at the small, high window overhead, then at the lean man reclining on the bunk. "How long we been in this place, Dave?"

Willoughby shoved the hat back from over his eyes. "I'd guess a little over half a day."

"Seems a passel longer than that."

"Patience, I gather, is not your strong suit."

Brubs snorted. "Buzzards got patience. All it gets 'em is rotten meat and a yard and a half of ugly apiece." He started pacing again.

"Relax, Brubs," Willoughby said, "you're wasting energy and tiring me out, tromping back and forth like that." He pulled the hat back over his eyes. "Better save your strength for that cotton patch."

Brubs paused to glare at the man on the cot. "You are truly a comfort to a dyin' man, Dave Willoughby. Truly a comfort."

The clomp of boots and the squeak of the door brought Brubs's pacing to a halt. Sheriff Milt Garrison strode to the cell, a big, burly man at his side. The big man seemed to wear more hair than a grizzly, Brubs thought. Gray fur covered most of his face, bristled his forearms, sprouted from heavy knuckles, and even stuck out through the buttonholes on his shirt. For a moment Brubs thought the man didn't have any eyes. Then he realized they were the same color as the hair and were tucked back under brows as thick and wiry as badger bristles.

"These the two Charlie told me about?" The hairy man's voice grated like a shovel blade against gravel.

"That's them." Milt Garrison leaned against the bars of the cell. "Told you they didn't look like much."

"Well, hell," the hairy one said, "if they're tough enough to wreck the Longhorn, maybe they'll do."

"Boys, meet Lawrence T. Pettibone, owner of Bexar and Rio Grande Freight Lines. He's got a deal to offer you." Garrison waved a hand toward the prisoners. "The short one's Brubs McCallan. Other one's Dave Willoughby."

Lawrence T. Pettibone nodded a greeting. "I hear you boys run up a pretty big bill last night. How bad you want to get shut of this place?"

"Mighty bad, Mr. Pettibone," Brubs said.

"All right, here's the deal. I won't say it but once, so you listen careful." Pettibone's smoky eyes seemed to turn harder, like a prize agate marble Brubs remembered from his childhood. "I need two men. You boys got horses and saddles?"

Brubs nodded. "Yes, sir, Mr. Pettibone, we sure do. Over at the livery."

Pettibone snorted. "Probably owe money on them, too."

"Yes, sir. I reckon we owe a dollar apiece board on the mounts."

"You savvy guns?"

Brubs nodded again. "Sure do. I'm a better'n fair hand with a long gun, and I can hit an outhouse with a pistol if it ain't too far off."

"How about you, Willoughby?"

Willoughby's brow wrinkled. "Yes, sir, I can use weapons. If the need arises." His tone sounded cautious.

Pettibone grunted. Brubs couldn't tell if it was a good grunt or a bad grunt. "All right, I guess you two'll do. I was hopin' for better, but a man can't be too picky these days." He pulled a twist of tobacco from a shirt pocket, gnawed off a chew, and settled it in his cheek. "I need two outriders. Guards for a shipment goin' to El Paso day after tomorrow. I'll pay your fines and damages. You ride shotgun for the Bexar and Rio line until you work it off. At a dollar a day."

Brubs sighed in relief. "Dave, that's twice the pay the county offered. And no hoe handles."

"Mr. Pettibone," Willoughby said, "may I inquire as to why you are short of manpower?"

Pettibone twisted his head and spat a wad of tobacco juice. It spanged neatly into a brass cuspidor below the lamp shelf. "Bandits killed 'em last run. Blew more holes in 'em than we could count. Stole my whole damn load."

"Bandits? You mean outlaws?"

Pettibone sighed in disgust. "Now just who the hell else would hold up a freight wagon? A gang of Methodist preachers?"

Willoughby shook his head warily. "I'm not sure about this, Mr. Pettibone. It's one thing to work for a man. It's another matter to possibly have to kill or be killed in the line of work."

Pettibone's gray eyes narrowed. "Suit yourself, son. It don't matter to me. But I need *two* men. Charlie said he figured you two come as a package. Guess I'll have to find me a couple other saddle tramps." He turned and started to walk away.

"Mr. Pettibone, wait a minute," Brubs called. He turned to Dave. "You leave the talkin' to me, Dave," he whispered. "I'm gettin' out of here, and you're goin' with me."

The big man turned back.

"My partner here ain't no lace-drawers type, Mr. Pettibone," Brubs said earnestly. "He's a top hand with a gun and got more guts than a bull buffalo. He just went through some stuff in the war that bothers him time to time. Don't you fret about old Dave." He clapped his cell mate on the shoulder. "You just get us out of here, and we'll make sure your wagon gets through."

Pettibone glared at the two prisoners for several heartbeats, then shrugged. "All right. You're hired." He jabbed a heavy finger at Brubs. "I want you boys to know one thing. I ain't in the charity business. You duck out or turn yellow on me and you'll wish to high hell you were back in this lockup, 'cause I'll skin you out and tan your hides for a pillow to ease my piles, and every time I go to the outhouse I'll take it along to remember you by. Savvy?"

"Yes, sir," Brubs said eagerly, "we savvy. You're the boss."

"Good. Keep that in mind. I'll pick you boys up tomorrow afternoon." He turned to walk away.

"Mr. Pettibone?"

"Now what, McCallan?"

Brubs swallowed. "Reckon you could get us out today? No disrespect to Bexar County or this fine sheriff here, but this ain't the most comfortable jail I ever been in. I sure would like to get my stuff in shape and take the kinks out of my sorrel before we move out."

Pettibone glowered at Brubs for a moment. "Damned if you boys don't try a man's patience something fierce. All right, I'll get you out now. You got any place to stay?"

"No, sir, Mr. Pettibone."

Pettibone's massive chest rose and fell. Brubs thought he saw the hair in the big man's ears bristle. "You can bunk in at my place. Cost you a dollar a day apiece. I'll add it onto what it's going to cost me to spring the pair of you. Damn, but the cost of help's gettin' high these days." Pettibone turned to the sheriff. "Cut 'em loose, Milt."

Brubs heaved a deep sigh of relief as the key turned in the cell lock and the barred door swung open. He knew it was the same air outside the cell as in, but it still smelled better. He and Willoughby fell into step behind the sheriff and Pettibone.

Brubs and Willoughby waited patiently as Lawrence T. Pettibone frowned at the column of figures on Sheriff Milt Garrison's ledger. "What the hell's this ten cents for a beer bottle?"

"Dave busted one over my head, Mr. Pettibone," Brubs said.

Pettibone snorted in disgust. "Damnedest thing I ever heard," he growled. "Chargin' a man for bustin' a beer bottle in a saloon brawl."

"Sort of the way I figured it, Mr. Pettibone," Brubs said earnestly. "Pricin' a man's fun plumb out of sight these days."

"I ain't payin' for no damn bottle," Pettibone said. "No way I can figure how to get ten cents worth of work out of two guys on a dollar a day."

Brubs dug in a pocket and produced a coin. "Give me a nickel, Dave. We'll split the cost of the bottle."

Pettibone finally grunted and pulled a wad of bills from his pocket. Brubs's eyes went wide at the sight of the roll. It was more money than he'd seen in one place since the big horse race up in Denton. Pettibone licked a thumb and counted out the bills, sighing as he caressed each one. Pettibone acted like he was burying a sainted mother every time he put a dollar on the desk, Brubs thought.

Garrison gathered up the bills, dropped the money in a tin box, and scribbled a receipt. He handed the paper to Pettibone, then retrieved the prisoners' weapons from a locked closet. "Guess you bought yourself some shotgun riders, Lawrence," he said.

Pettibone cast a cold glance at Brubs and Willoughby. "Don't know if I bought a good horse or a wind-broke plug," he groused. "I sure as hell hope they ride and shoot better than they smell. You boys are a touch ripe. There's a big water tank out by my wagon barn. Wouldn't hurt either of you to nuzzle up to some soap. Now, strap them gun belts on and let's go bail your horses out of the lockup."

Willoughby paused for a moment, rotated the cylinder of his Colt, and raised an eyebrow. "Should we go ahead and load the chambers now, Mr. Pettibone?" he asked.

Pettibone groaned aloud. "Fools. I just bought two idiots with my hard-earned money. Dammit, son, what good's an unloaded pistol?" He watched in disgust as Willoughby thumbed cartridges into the Colt and reached for his Winchester rifle. "I guess you boys got plenty of ammunition?"

"I got ten rifle cartridges," Brubs said, shoving loads into his scarred Henry .44 rimfire long gun. "Maybe a dozen for the pistol."

"I have half a box of .44-40's," Willoughby said. "Same caliber fits both my handgun and rifle."

Pettibone snorted in disgust. "Damn. Now I've got to lay out some more hard cash on you two. My men don't ride with less than a hundred rounds each. Come on—we'll stop off at the general store down the street."

The two men fell into step behind Pettibone. A few minutes later the hairy one emerged from the store, four boxes of ammunition in a big hand. "I'll add the cost of the shells to your bill, boys. Fifty cents a box."

"Fifty cents? Mr. Pettibone, that's a dime more than I paid anywhere," Brubs said, incredulous.

"Call it a nuisance fee," Pettibone growled, "because you boys are nuisance if I ever seen 'em. Course, if you'd rather work it out with the county—"

"No, sir," Brubs said quickly. "I reckon that's fair enough. We won't nuisance you no more."

"I doubt that." Pettibone spat a wad of used-up tobacco into the street. "Let's get home before you two drifters cost me my last dollar."

"Mr. Pettibone?"

"What now, McCallan?"

"Any chance we could get a bottle of whiskey added to our bill?"

"No, by God!" Pettibone bellowed. "Don't push your luck, boy, or you'll be behind a hoe handle all summer!"

"Yes, sir," Brubs said. "But it was worth a try."

A half hour later, Brubs and Willoughby rode side by side behind Lawrence T. Pettibone's buggy. Brubs forked a big, rangy sorrel, and Dave rode a leggy black that looked to have some Tennessee racing stock in his bloodline.

"Brubs," Willoughby quietly, "I have the distinct impression that our new employer is somewhat thrifty with his funds."

Brubs flashed a quick grin. "I reckon he can squeeze a peso until the Mexican eagle looks like a plucked crow."

Lawrence T. Pettibone's combination home and wagon yard and adjoining stock pastures spread over most of a section on the northern outskirts of San Antonio.

Brubs had to admit he was impressed. The corrals were sturdy, fenced by peeled logs the size of a man's thigh, and watered by a big windmill that creaked as it whirred in the southwest breeze. The barn was as solidly built as the corrals, expansive and well-ventilated. The main house was big, and built of real cut lumber, not adobe or split logs.

Brubs was even more impressed with what came from inside the big house.

Pettibone pushed the door open, growled at Brubs and Willoughby to wait on the porch, and went inside. He was back a minute later with a stiff-bristled brush and a bar of lye soap in hand, and one of the prettiest girls Brubs had seen west of Savannah trailing behind.

The girl was blond. Palomino hair tumbled past her shoulders, dancing gold in the warm afternoon sunshine. The pale rose housedress she wore wrapped itself around a figure that made Brubs want to paw the ground and snort. Her eyes were big, blue, and had a smoldering look about them above a perky, upturned nose. She looked to be about twenty. This, Brubs knew instinctively, was one hot-blooded woman. He swept the battered and stained hat from his head.

"Boys, this here is Callie, my daughter," Pettibone said. "Callie, these two bums'll be riding shotgun for us a spell. Don't shoot 'em for prowlers until I get my money back out of 'em. The little feller's name is Brubs McCallan. The tall one's Dave Willoughby."

Brubs bowed deep at the waist, then grinned at the blonde. He wished for a moment he had just had a bath and shave; some women were mighty picky about that, as if it made some sort of difference. "Mighty pleased to make your acquaintance, Miss Pettibone," Brubs said. "A pretty girl does brighten a poor saddle tramp's day."

"Lay a hand on Callie and I'll kill you," Pettibone said. It wasn't exactly a threat, Brubs noted. More like a statement of fact.

Brubs tore his gaze from the girl and glanced at his cell mate. Willoughby had removed his hat, but merely nodded a greeting. He did not speak.

A second woman, a Mexican somewhere in her late twenties, appeared at the door. She was a bit thick of hip and waist, her upper lip dusted by scattered but distinct black hairs. Overall though, not bad looking, Brubs decided. Away from the blonde she might even be pretty.

"That's Juanita. She's the cook and maid." Pettibone held out the brush and lye soap. "Long as I'm makin' introductions this is stuff to clean up with. Put your horses in the barn and yourselves in that water tank out back, or don't come in for supper."

Brubs hesitated, reluctant to leave the warm glow that seemed to spread in all directions from Callie, until he realized that Lawrence T. Pettibone was glaring a hole through him. Brubs quickly replaced his hat, turned away, and mounted with a flourish, swinging into the saddle without touching a stirrup. He wasn't above showing off a bit when a pretty girl was watching. He kneed his sorrel gelding around and set off after Willoughby, who was already leading his leggy black toward the barn thirty yards away.

"Man, ain't she something?" Brubs said as he reined in alongside Willoughby. "I ain't seen a filly like that my whole life through. Prime stuff, that Callie."

Willoughby cast a worried glance at Brubs. "You heard what Pettibone said, Brubs. You'd better leave the girl alone."

Brubs chuckled aloud. "Just adds a little spice to the puddin', my Yankee friend. You see the way Callie was lookin' at me? Her eyes got all smoky-like."

"I saw the way Pettibone was looking at you." Willoughby swung the corral gate open.

"Ah, that inflated tadpole ain't much to worry about," Brubs said.

"I worry about a lot of things, Brubs. One of which is that if you try messing around with that girl, somebody is likely to get hurt. Like you and me."

Brubs reached down and cuffed Dave on the shoulder. "Don't you fret, Dave. You just watch ol' Brubs work that herd, you'll learn somethin' about handlin' women."

"And that," Willoughby said solemnly, "is exactly what's bothering me. I'm beginning to wonder if perhaps Brubs McCallan wasn't put on this earth just to get one Dave Willoughby killed."

If you enjoyed this book, subscribe now and get...

TWO FREE

A $7.00 VALUE–

If you would like to read more of the very best, most exciting, adventurous, action-packed Westerns being published today, you'll want to subscribe to True Value's Western Home Subscription Service.

Each month the editors of True Value will select the 6 very best Westerns from America's leading publishers for special readers like you. You'll be able to preview these new titles as soon as they are published, *FREE* for ten days with no obligation!

TWO FREE BOOKS

When you subscribe, we'll send you your first month's shipment of the newest and best 6 Westerns for you to preview. With your first shipment, two of these books will be yours as our introductory gift to you absolutely *FREE* (a $7.00 value), regardless of what you decide to do. If you like them, as much as we think you will, keep all six books but pay for just 4 at the low subscriber rate of just $2.75 each. If you decide to return them, keep 2 of the titles as our gift. No obligation.

Special Subscriber Savings

When you become a True Value subscriber you'll save money several ways. First, all regular monthly selections will be billed at the low subscriber price of just $2.75 each. That's at least a savings of $4.50 each month below the publishers price. Second, there is never any shipping, handling or other hidden charges—*Free home delivery*. What's more there is no minimum number of books you must buy, you may return any selection for full credit and you can cancel your subscription at any time. A TRUE VALUE!

A special offer for people who enjoy reading the best Westerns published today.

WESTERNS!

NO OBLIGATION

Mail the coupon below

To start your subscription and receive 2 FREE WESTERNS, fill out the coupon below and mail it today. We'll send your first shipment which includes 2 FREE BOOKS as soon as we receive it.

Mail To: **True Value Home Subscription Services, Inc. P.O. Box 5235
120 Brighton Road, Clifton, New Jersey 07015-5235**

YES! I want to start reviewing the very best Westerns being published today. Send me my first shipment of 6 Westerns for me to preview FREE for 10 days. If I decide to keep them, I'll pay for just 4 of the books at the low subscriber price of $2.75 each; a total $11.00 (a $21.00 value). Then each month I'll receive the 6 newest and best Westerns to preview Free for 10 days. If I'm not satisfied I may return them within 10 days and owe nothing. Otherwise I'll be billed at the special low subscriber rate of $2.75 each; a total of $16.50 (at least a $21.00 value) and save $4.50 off the publishers price. There are never any shipping, handling or other hidden charges. I understand I am under no obligation to purchase any number of books and I can cancel my subscription at any time, no questions asked. In any case the 2 FREE books are mine to keep.

Name

Street Address   Apt. No.

City   State   Zip Code

Telephone

Signature
(if under 18 parent or guardian must sign)

Terms and prices subject to change. Orders subject
to acceptance by True Value Home Subscription
Services, Inc.

14128-4

JAKE LOGAN

TODAY'S HOTTEST ACTION WESTERN!

_SLOCUM'S WAR (Giant Novel)	0-425-13273-0/$3.99
_DEATH'S HEAD TRAIL #161	0-425-13335-4/$3.50
_SILVER TOWN SHOWDOWN #162	0-425-13359-1/$3.99
_SLOCUM AND THE BUSHWHACKERS #163	0-425-13401-6/$3.99
_SLOCUM AND THE WYOMING FRAME-UP #164	0-425-13472-5/$3.99
_SAN ANGELO SHOOTOUT #165	0-425-13508-X/$3.99
_BLOOD FEVER #166	0-425-13532-2/$3.99
_HELLTOWN TRAIL #167	0-425-13579-9/$3.99
_SHERIFF SLOCUM #168	0-425-13624-8/$3.99
_VIRGINIA CITY SHOWDOWN #169	0-425-13761-9/$3.99
_SLOCUM AND THE FORTY THIEVES #170	0-425-13797-X/$3.99
_POWDER RIVER MASSACRE #171	0-425-13665-5/$3.99
_SLOCUM AND THE TIN STAR SWINDLE #173	0-425-13811-9/$3.99
_SLOCUM AND THE NIGHTRIDERS #174	0-425-13839-9/$3.99
_REVENGE AT DEVILS TOWER #175	0-425-13904-2/$3.99
_SLOCUM AT OUTLAWS' HAVEN #176	0-425-13951-4/$3.99
_AMBUSH AT APACHE ROCKS #177	0-425-13981-6/$3.99
_HELL TO MIDNIGHT #178	0-425-14010-5/$3.99
_SLOCUM AND THE BUFFALO SOLDIERS #179	0-425-14050-4/$3.99
_SLOCUM AND THE PHANTOM GOLD #180	0-425-14100-4/$3.99
_GHOST TOWN #181	0-425-14128-4/$3.99
_SLOCUM & THE INVADERS #182 (April)	0-425-14182-9/$3.99

Payable in U.S. funds. No cash orders accepted. Postage & handling: $1.75 for one book, 75¢ for each additional. Maximum postage $5.50. Prices, postage and handling charges may change without notice. Visa, Amex, MasterCard call 1-800-788-6262, ext. 1, refer to ad # 202c

Or, check above books and send this order form to:
The Berkley Publishing Group
390 Murray Hill Pkwy., Dept. B
East Rutherford, NJ 07073

Bill my: ☐ Visa ☐ MasterCard ☐ Amex _____ (expires)

Card#_____

($15 minimum)

Signature_____

Please allow 6 weeks for delivery.   Or enclosed is my: ☐ check ☐ money order

Name_____

Address_____

City_____

State/ZIP_____

Book Total $_____
Postage & Handling $_____
Applicable Sales Tax $_____
(NY, NJ, PA, CA, GST Can.)
Total Amount Due $_____